Rise of th

a prequel to
Sons of Iberia

by

J. Glenn Bauer

Prologue

In a land of sun-ripened scents, fire, and sand, spears rose high in salute. Gripped in hands that varied in hue from pale skinned to those stained dark by generations of sun. The warriors of a dozen nations cheered as one, their voices thick with excitement, and eyes alight with the joy of adventure.

With the wind at their backs, the galleys offloaded these same warriors on the shores of southern Iberia. Men, shouts of challenge on their lips, leaped from ships to land in shallow surf and lumber onto the sand and rock. Horses were plunged into the water from fat bellied cargo ships and made to swim ashore while sacks and crates of provisions were rowed to the beach in smaller vessels.

All this activity did not go unnoticed. Eyes watched from the cliffs and from the tree line. Blades were whetted and bows strung. The people of this land were used to victory. They were numerous and rich. Their weapons and shields had stood their ancestors in good stead and would soon be singing again with the joy of battle. The people of this part of Iberia were the Turdetani. Feared and hated by the neighbouring tribes, the Turdetani rejoiced in battle.

That joy and their battle lust wore thin in just one season as the warriors from across the sea stood firm time after time against their wild assaults. Villages were burned and the walls of towns that had not been breached in living memory fell.

Now warriors retreated to the hills or packed the possessions of kin and clan onto wagons and travelled north or west, leaving behind them those that bent their heads and laid down their blades at their enemy's feet.

Hamilcar Barca, general of the victorious army, watched as tributes piled up, brought to him by the graybeards and leading men of the Turdetani. He lifted a dull gray ingot from a crate containing many more like it. Hefting it, his smile grew until his teeth shone through his oiled beard. His eyes followed the train of wagons back to the far distant hills that lay in the north and he grinned.

Chapter 1

Stones and dirt rattled down a cleft gouged by winter rains into the face of the hill. As suddenly as they had started falling, they stopped and into the silence came a hissed curse. A bloodied hand appeared from a thicket, parting the branches to reveal a man in a torn tunic and battered leather armour. With a pained jerk, he stepped from cover and stood swaying, his sunken eyes fixed on two youths frozen in their tracks below him.

Dubgetious swallowed and looked closer at the man. "Father? Father!"

The second youth gave a cry of fear, dropped a half-butchered hare and fled back towards the village. Dubgetious called after him, but the youth never slowed. He turned back and scrambled up the steep slope, reaching for his father who clung weakly to a tree.

"Father! You are injured." Dubgetious' voice failed as he looked closer at the bloodied man, a warrior champion of their clan of Bastetani. The stench of shit and spew that rose from him was enough to cause the youth's stomach to rebel. Worse was the purple gut that protruded from a gaping wound in the man's side, like the tongue of a crucified criminal.

From a distance, cries of dismay floated into the afternoon air. Dubgetious' companion had no doubt reached their village. His father's eyes stretched wide and his crusted lips parted.

"Dubgetious. You must flee." The words scraped between broken teeth and bloodied lips like a blade on a whetstone.

Stepping forward, Dubgetious gripped his father's arm and eased his shoulder under it, wrapping the limb over his own broad shoulders. Taller than the champion, Dubgetious easily took up his father's weight as the man grunted and went limp.

Villagers crowded around him on the narrow path as he made his way to the village gates, his father staggering at his side. The first of them had cursed at the sight of Venza's wounds, then followed others who wept when they saw who it was Dubgetious bore.

A thin-faced man with weeping sores stippling his throat, stepped in front of Dubgetious forcing him to stop. The man spat at Dubgetious' feet and spoke to his father.

"Venza, you led our warriors away to battle with spears held high and words bright with victory. Where now are our Spears?" The man's face darkened as he stared at the limp warrior slumped against Dubgetious. Without a care for the man's wounds, he lunged and grabbed Venza by his matted hair, lifting his face. "Where is my wife? My son?" Both had marched with Venza ten days earlier.

Dubgetious growled at the man who silenced him with a cold glare. A woman called to the man to release the wounded champion.

With a frustrated snarl, the man cursed and turned, shouldering through the crowd. Dubgetious resumed his path, leaving behind grim faced women and men who stared into the setting sun, their hopes of seeing their kin fading.

The village occupied a hilltop and was encircled by a thick wall of packed rock and sharpened stakes as thick around as a warrior's thigh. Smoke from cook fires smeared the sky above the settlement. Goats bleated as they were driven from the surrounding hills to be milked and hounds fought running battles in the dry scrub, their mood infected by the tension of the villagers.

Dubgetious licked his lips as he bent under his father's weight and sent a hurried prayer to Endovex to allow his father to heal. With a grunt, he dragged Venza through the gates and towards their house of timber and stone.

Men and women parted before him and even the most brazen of children fell silent as he staggered on, sweat beading his brow and his breathing laboured. A pair of hands appeared, lifting his father's right arm and sharing the burden.

Dubgetious' eyes slid to the young woman. "Thank you, 'Ratza."

"He is a graybeard and they shun him." Beratza directed her words at the watching people, her eyes flashing with anger.

"Do not, please." Dubgetious whispered. Only one summer his elder, she feared no one and spoke her mind as she pleased.

"They sicken me." Her voiced softened. "He is sore injured, Dubgetious."

Dubgetious clenched his teeth, his eyes fixed on the curtain that hung slack across the door to his home. Three more paces and he kicked open a gate of woven saplings and edged his father's body through the curtain.

Once they had lowered him to the rushes in the centre of the small room, Dubgetious sat back on his haunches with a grunt, his eyes wide and hands shaking. Beratza was already pulling items from the bleached wood shelves where his mother stored sweet herbs and foul unguents. He wiped his brow and caught sight of his hand. It was smeared thick with gore.

Beratza saw. "There is going to be more of that. Better go fetch vinegar and bring the Herb Queen."

Dubgetious looked at his father's form, spread across the floor, his chest rising in short jerks before subsiding with a gurgle.

"Lyda will kill him if he dies."

"He will die if you stand there like a tree. Go!"

Ducking his head, the tall Bastetani youth stepped into the coming night, his mind fogged with the dust of wild fears. He felt eyes on him and noticed the sullen, fearful faces of neighbours standing in clusters between their small beehive shaped homes. He hawked and spat to rid his mouth of the taste of the stench from the festering wounds his father carried. Stepping between homes and angling uphill, he quickly made his way to the circle of buildings at the centre of the village used to store the village oils, cereals and cured meats. Three warriors guarded the stores and the tallest of them nodded to him when he stopped in the light shed by their brazier.

"Greetings, Silban. I need an amphora of vinegar." Dubgetious at just fifteen years old, stood as tall as the warriors and looked the tallest in the eye.

The man studied Dubgetious for a heartbeat before nodding to one of his fellows. "Fetch it for the lad." A warrior grunted and went off into the deepening twilight.

Silban nodded. "I saw the wounds, lad. I will send a plea to Endovex. Did he say what happened?"

"His only words were that we should flee." He looked into the guard's eyes. "Perhaps the enemy is nearby?"

The man lifted his bearded chin and stared into the night for a long moment as though trying to pierce the smoky darkness with his old eyes.

"Should we flee, do you think?" He directed at his fellow guard.

The man belched contemptuously before speaking. "Never did before. Leave that kind of thing to the Turdetani or Oretani."

The third guard appeared out of the gloom with an amphora swinging in his hand. He thrust it at Dubgetious. "I made your father's mark against the tally."

"Thank you." Dubgetious felt the cold of the liquid seeping through the fired clay and turned away.

"If Lyda needs a hand when she returns, you tell her I, Silban, am a friend." The warrior called after him.

Dubgetious walked faster, his face stiff. Dodging villagers in the narrow confines between their homes, he quickly reached the house of the village healer, the Herb Queen. The curtain at her doorway was knotted shut, indicating she was not inside. Dubgetious cursed and returned quickly to his home where he heard voices from behind the curtained entrance. Light flared around its edges and a man groaned. He hurried forward and whipped the curtain aside to see the Herb Queen crouched low beside Venza's naked form. Beratza knelt at Venza's head, her knees bracing his head and her sinewy arms pinning his wrists to the floor.

"'Ratza? What are you doing?"

"Help her hold him!" The Herb Queen ordered, never taking her eyes from the inflamed bulge in the warrior's side. She spat a wad of chewed green unguent directly onto the wound. Dubgetious set down the amphora and quickly grabbed at his father's writhing legs, pinning his ankles and pressing down on the man's knees.

"I brought the vinegar." He offered.

The Herb Queen's stained fingers pushed wadding down over the protruding gut, eliciting another deep moan from Venza. Dubgetious was hard-pressed to hold his father's legs still, and he eyed Beratza to be sure she could cope with his arms.

"He is god-favoured. I smell no shit from his gut in the wound." The herb queen worked deft fingers into the slash and hooked out a clot of bloody tunic. "Still, best to use the vinegar now that you have brought it."

She cast an eye at Dubgetious and he quickly averted his gaze, staring at his father's shuddering chest. She rose and slid past him, sleek thighs brushing his shoulder, the smell of her goading a response from his body.

He glanced at Beratza who watched him with a knowing grin.

She hitched her eyebrows and his smile flashed before he caught it and returned to staring at the grievous wound.

The sharp odour of vinegar filled the air when the Herb Queen struck off the wax stopper on the amphora.

"Your father took most of our best Spears with him." The Herb Queen spoke from behind him and then pressed past him and crouched once again beside Venza, the unsealed amphora tucked beneath an arm. She made no move to tend to the man's wounds, but gazed at Dubgetious.

"They may still return." His voice was hollow.

"He will tell you when he wakes, but I will say it now; they are slain." She made a gesture to ward off the shades of those who might haunt her.

Dubgetious looked at Beratza, who scowled back at him. Turning to the Herb Queen he shrugged.

"Without those Spears we will be overcome. Why are you so certain they are slain? Is that your wish?" His tone hardened as he spoke.

The corner of the Herb Queen's lip lifted and the black orbs at the centre of her brown eyes widened. "The pup has some sack! Good!" She grinned a generous smile of white teeth stark behind full, tawny coloured lips. "You will need a warrior's sack for you must take this news to Batrun. Tonight."

Dubgetious reared back, forgetting his grip on Venza's ankles. "Not I!" He glanced at Venza who lay unmoving now apart from the rise and fall of his chest and the twitch of his sunken eyelids. "Who are you to tell me to do this thing?"

Beratza hissed at his words, but the Herb Queen gestured to her to remain silent, her eyes never leaving Dubgetious' own.

"I tell you because by tomorrow the others will have convinced themselves all will be well." She spat. "It will not be. The same knives that cut your father will be coming to flay us all."

"Batrun though? He is not even Bastetani." Dubgetious protested.

"He may as well be. For seven seasons he has been called graybeard by the Bastetani warriors he leads." She grimaced as wind leaked from Venza's body and swiftly began dousing the wound with vinegar.

The blade that had opened his gut had pierced the man's right arm and again the shoulder. Beratza, oblivious to the acrid stink of the piss-coloured vinegar, began washing the crusted blood and gore from these wounds.

Dubgetious rose and fetched a length of linen to gird about his father's loins. As he did so, he was conscious of the Herb Queen's attention on him. Bristling, he refused to raise his eyes to her. For long heartbeats they worked, Beratza cleaning the wounds and the Herb Queen packing them with chewed poultice. Dubgetious dabbed ineffectively at the growing pool of blood and vinegar accumulating between the rushes.

"It will take me two days to reach the clans that Batrun speaks for. What message shall I give him?"

Dubgetious' heart beat fast and his hands were clammy with nerves at the prospect of delivering a message to the warrior. He knew the Herb Queen's words were wise and that soon the wolves that hunted for the Barca from Carthage would be howling at their gates. Warriors and graybeards would be needed. He dropped the filthy cloth and sat back on his haunches, letting his eyes roam the Herb Queen's lithe form, her supple thighs exposed as she crouched, a firm breast that pulled against the sleeveless tunic and the curve of her throat. He and 'Ratza had unclothed one another and done some adventurous fondling on a handful of occasions and Dubgetious could imagine happily doing the same with the Herb Queen.

"I have roots that are longer than your little spear, pup." Her words came from a distance and stirred his fantasy. The next shattered them. "The roots I speak of will soften you for all time."

Dubgetious jerked as though awaking from a trance and saw Beratza smirking and the Herb Queen's eyes hard on him.

He cleared his throat hastily. "What message? For Batrun?"

She turned her palm up over Venza's body. "Perhaps that we have no warriors left to field? That our champion lies pierced through?"

"But what shall I ask of him? That he should send his Spears to man our walls?" Dubgetious shrank from her look and he grunted as her meaning became clear. "That we will pay him a tithe then for protection."

She smiled, transforming again. "More than just sack then. That is right, Dubgetious."

He felt heat rise through the skin of his throat and cheeks at her use of his name. It set his heart beating faster and he forced himself to nod slowly as he had seen his father do when considering grave matters.

"I shall prepare for the journey. A waterskin. No, two."

"I have done what I can. Your father will last the night." She rose to her feet. "Take a midden heap for all I care, just be sure you set off before the moon rises." She vanished through the curtain, leaving it swaying gently behind her.

Chapter 2

Seven times the sun had risen and still the Barca's wolves had not come. Neither had the Spears promised by Batrun. A long night guarding the gates had left Dubgetious weary and his father still lay weakly in his cot. A stench rose from his skin, more bitter than the meanest sour wine and his stools were loose and black, as was the piss that leaked from his ever-shrinking manhood. After cleaning the mess and dribbling a thin gruel between his father's lips, Dubgetious had no desire to take to his cot and breathe the odour, instead he took up a blanket and went outside to await the rising sun.

He stirred from where he rested with his back against the slowly warming stone wall. His feet had blistered on the arduous journey to the home of the clan of Batrun. They had bled as he raced home. Now, after two days of hobbling, they stung less and he considered walking to the gates to stretch his stiffening legs. He closed his eyes and let his head fall back, recollecting the night he had stepped before the Carthaginian who had turned Bastetani.

The man was truly a graybeard, for Dubgetious had never seen a beard as thick nor long as the shovel of hair that curled beneath the man's chin.

He had delivered the news of the unseen deaths of their clan's Spears and of his father's wounds. Batrun had nodded sombrely at the news while his leading men had ceased their drinking to exchange glances and grins. Dubgetious had felt fury then. He clenched his fists even now as he thought of how they had dishonoured the dead. His indignation had earned him a sound kicking at the feet of Batrun's warriors. When they had finished, and he was a curled ball of bruises, he had cracked an eye to see Batrun grinning at him.

The graybeard had promised the Spears needed to hold the walls and then sent Dubgetious to sleep among the goats on an empty belly.

Sandaled feet slapped closer and Dubgetious roused himself and squinted against the glare of the early morning sun. Beratza was running up the hill, her hair bouncing like a horse's mane at her shoulders, muscular thighs flashing. She clutched a spear in her killing hand and a round shield in her left.

"Dubgetious! Your spear!"

He rolled to his feet, uncaring of the raw blisters. In a heartbeat, he was through the curtain to snatch his spear from the rafters and slip his feet into his sandals, tramping the leather straps beneath his heels.

"Dubgetious!"

"Coming!" His shield was splintered and he had not made time to repair it. Cursing, he batted aside the curtain to hear the familiar blaring of Bastetani warhorns echo from the hills. The sound lifted the hairs on his arms and he shivered.

"Batrun's Spears!"

Batrun came that day. Dubgetious watched the sun glint off a thousand spear points dipping and rustling like a field of iron-tipped grass as they made their way to the village. The warriors were led by Batrun himself. The man rode a barrel-chested mount and was dressed as a champion should be. His feet enclosed by thick fleece and heavy sandals laced to the knees. His padded tunic reached to his thighs and gray chain hung from his shoulders to below his waist where it was cinched tight by a wide leather belt studded with bronze. His head was crowned by a helmet of worked iron and from under its rim, his eyes glowed with dark intensity.

Dubgetious' chest expanded with admiration and he gripped his spear tighter. This was a war leader! This was a champion that could create a victory and at his back were the Spears that would win that victory and stop the Barca.

The watching villagers and refugee warriors from the west felt the same and their loud whoops and cheers were accompanied by the deep drumming of spear hafts on shields.

"That is Batrun? You went before him and spoke our oath to him?" Beratza's voice was breathless and Dubgetious thought he detected a note of approval there.

"I did. The four warriors at his back kicked the shades out of me while he watched." He grinned at her, making her laugh and slap his uncovered head.

"We can win against this Hamilcar with Batrun as our champion, Dubgetious. The Bastetani can lead all other tribes, even the far distant Vettones and Illerget."

The village was awash with bodies in every passage, at every doorway, and even among the goats in their pens. Dubgetious stumbled over an unseen limb and heard a grunt from beneath a bundle of furs and leather. He suppressed the urge to throw up and made quickly for the village well. There were few others stirring and those that were, groaned and retched were they lay, ill from the flagons of ale consumed in celebration the night before.

"Greetings, Dubgetious." The Herb Queen's voice pulled his head around to where she stood beneath an ancient apple tree.

"Greetings. You have not come to see Venza." He accused her, his mood darkening.

"He will live till he dies." She lifted her hand, stilling his retort, and stepped close to him. Dubgetious wanted to back away from her, conscious of the reek of fermented ale on his breath, but was held in place by her presence. "You smell worse than he." Her nose wrinkled.

"Then you have seen him. My apologies."

She grunted, suddenly impatient. "Take Beratza and go find your mother."

"Why? She prefers her own company and that of her Spears." The Herb Queen's face remained impassive, but Dubgetious was sure he saw a tightening about her eyes.

He grinned. "Anyway, I am not going anywhere before we have defeated the Barca." His grin faltered when the Herb Queen's eyes flashed. "Batrun is a champion, and just look at the number of spears he has."

She looked west, past the town walls and to the hills painted in early morning gold. Her jaw clenched, muscles bunching beneath the shells dangling from her pierced earlobes.

"The enemy will be here before the sun clears the hills. Not even Batrun and all his spears can stop them, but you Dubgetious can save Beratza. She will go if you do."

Dubgetious' eyes widened as he understood. The Herb Queen and Beratza?

Shaking his head at the image, he stuttered, "Wait, the enemy, Barca? How do you know?"

She gestured to the gates, where for the first time, Dubgetious noticed there was a fire burning and a circle of warriors seated, as though in negotiation.

"Bastetani came from the west in the night. They flee the jaws of the enemy who they say snap at their heels."

"I cannot go. I owe my father and my people my spear and my blood if the gods ask it." He flinched at the sorrow he saw shadowed in her eyes, certain suddenly that his own sorrows were about to engulf him.

The sun, reaching still for the highest point of the sky, cast a ruddy glow through thick smoke. Dubgetious felt his vision swim and his heart beat like a hammer at his ribs. It filled his nostrils forcing a hacking cough between his parched lips. A figure leaped through a fresh cloud of hot, roiling smoke with a battle cry, spear stabbing forward and then flicking left and right. Dubgetious fell back, trying to lift his own spear which weighed as much as a tree in his tired arms. Beratza, bloodied and grunting, threw a rock that struck the large Turdetani warrior's shoulder. The man laughed, dark eyes glinting savagely under thick eyebrows.

Screams washed through Dubgetious and he shook at the horrors glimpsed through the curtains of smoke. The mounds of bloodied heaps at the foot of the village walls. The cataracts of crimson washing down the stone stairs leading from the village centre. There was more and Dubgetious' eyes skittered over the scenes of butchery and violence, his young mind trying to make sense of it.

He stabbed at the Turdetani whose hungry eyes were locked on Beratza. The point of his blade took him in the groin and with a supreme grunt, Dubgetious used the last strength of his broad shoulders to twist the blade and open the thick blood vessel there.

More figures flowed around him and a club took him in the head, exploding a wash of searing pain across his vision. He fell to the stones and came face to face with Beratza. Her eyes were wild as she fought off groping hands and then widened in horror at some worse pain inflicted on her.

The survivors were forced to their knees, Dubgetious amongst them. The youth watched through cloudy eyes as warriors dragged survivors from under piles of dead where they had crawled to hide. A girl was pulled by her ankles from a midden heap, her body black with goat shit and bruises. A warrior, her arm ending at a hand turned to shattered bone and ground flesh, was harassed from a narrow passage between the Bastetani homes and into the circle of captives. A blow to her knee dropped her beside Dubgetious. Silence of a kind settled over the defeated village. From the distance, came the sound of occasional clashes as the Barca's huge army hunted Batrun's surviving Spears.

Hooves clattered on stone and a band of riders appeared, led by a large man with a distinctive curled beard. He wore the armour of a wealthy warrior and the symbol of the Carthaginian's deity was vivid on his shield. Without preamble the warrior spoke, his voice loud and clear.

"Bastetani! You would have been wiser to submit at once." He leaned forward and his eyes locked on Dubgetious. "Tanit has favoured you and spared your lives. From this day forward you will consider Carthage as your protector and you will answer her call through my voice, for I am Hamilcar Barca of Carthage." With an agility that belied the gray in his beard, he sprang from his mount. "All the warriors here today will march now as levies in my army."

The woman beside Dubgetious growled and tried to surge to her feet. Dubgetious reached out and grabbed for her shoulder. Too late.

"Do not!" He hissed.

A dark-skinned warrior noticed and darted at them, his sword a blur. Dubgetious fell back as the blade whipped down and bit into the woman's neck. Its keen edge was dulled by a morning of killing and the warrior wrenched it free to hack again while the woman's eyes rolled back into her head at the pain of the ghastly wound. He struck four times before she slumped across Dubgetious' knees, her blood arcing across his chest.

Hamilcar Barca watched impassively. "As brave as any warrior I know. That is why I want your Spears to serve with me. Together we can forge a new alliance that benefits your people greatly. Resist and in a short while the hills and villages will be filled only with the shades of Bastetani!"

Dubgetious lifted his eyes from the woman's face and stared at the Barca who strode towards him. A blade touched Dubgetious' neck and the dark-skinned warrior warned him not to move, speaking a dialect of Greek used in trade ports the sea over.

"I will not." Dubgetious answered, his voice steady.

"You speak Greek, young warrior?" Hamilcar addressed him.

"I do." Dubgetious drew his shoulders back and raised his chin, oblivious to the threat of the blade still at his neck.

"Remove your blade, Keneiss." Hamilcar instructed the warrior. "What is your name, son?"

"I am Dubgetious of the Bastetani, son of Venza."

"Your father fought here today? Does he live still?" Hamilcar asked.

Dubgetious shook his head, but a voice, guttural with pain and sickness, croaked from among the captives.

"I am and I am pleased to say I blooded my spear today." Dubgetious started as Venza's head rose above those of the kneeling captives.

Hamilcar took in the man's waxen face and sweating, shivering body. "You killed even as you hover at the brink of death." Hamilcar spread his arms wide and turned in a circle, addressing all. "Truly the Bastetani are an honourable and brave people. I, Hamilcar Barca, offer you my hand in friendship from this day forth if you would but take it."

Venza grunted and looked across bowed heads at Dubgetious, eyes shining with fever. Dubgetious felt a prickle of pride and his eyes filled rapidly with tears as his father nodded once before he toppled to the ground.

Hamilcar Barca stood watching the broken captives who held their faces low and kept their shoulders bent. The encircling warriors moved restlessly as heartbeats passed with no sign of the Bastetani captives taking the Barca's offer. Spears lifted and swords rasped. Bloodied warriors sated with killing looked at one another, preparing for a final orgy of butchery.

Hamilcar Barca's hands dropped slowly, clenching into fists at his sides. With eyes hardening by the moment, he looked around a final time and then leaped astride his mount. A fellow rider passed him a heavy spear and the Barca couched it in the crook of his elbow and turned his horse. A sigh rose from the bowed captives, men women and children who knew the blades would fall on them now and send their shades hurtling into the land of Saur and his hounds, the land of the god of death.

"I will." Dubgetious gripped the blade at his neck with his fist and pushed it away. He rose, allowing the dead warrior's body to slide off his lap, forcing back the dark-skinned warrior holding the sword. All heads turned to him, warriors and captives alike. "I will accept the friendship of Carthage and Barca. My spear is yours."

Chapter 3

Her shoulders were tight with tension as she led the small column of seven riders along the hillside, keeping shy of the ridge. She flicked a look up at the black smoke that rose from the next valley, worry lines around her eyes deepening.

"The smoke is thinning, Lyda." A lanky warrior gestured at it.

"Maybe there was just a mishap and only a roof or two burned."

Lyda grunted, unconvinced. The warrior had a wife in the village, heavy with child. He was holding onto the hope that they were safe. Lyda had seen villages pillaged in raids and burned by attackers. The smoke was thinning, but the flames that had lifted it had burned more than thatch. She knew it and soon the warrior would as well. Her eyes swept the ridge and found the boulder that marked the trail they would use to descend to the village and discover its fate. At that moment, her mount skittered to the side and snorted. Lyda hissed and lifted her shield, trusting the horse's keen senses. Behind her, other mounts reacted similarly, causing their riders to curse.

"There!" She pointed into the valley that fell away to their right. The riders pulled their mounts to a stop, eyes squinting through the thickets of thorn and bush that grew lower down. A flurry of black wings was accompanied by raucous cries as a pair of ravens circled and then dived.

The dead numbered just a handful. All were stripped and mutilated. Crimson wounds vivid against the white of skin usually covered by clothing.

"These are not ours, but I recognise him." The warrior gestured at the body of a man that lay amongst a nest of boulders, his head twisted unnaturally. "He is one of Batrun's leading men. I think the lad there with his guts around his throat was his son."

Lyda was silent, her lips pressed thin and her eyes hard as flint. "We can come back and put them to the pyre. First, we need to return to our home and see what has been wrought in our absence." She looked long at the hard men and women that sat their mounts beside her and saw them steel themselves for what they might find.

Descending the hillside, Lyda could see the maze of stone homes and fenced livestock pens within the village walls. She saw the burned thatch of a handful of houses, but she also saw figures moving among the buildings. Her heart lifted with hope which faded again as they circled the walls to enter the gates.
There had been a hard battle here. The ground was trampled and rutted. Discarded sandals, torn cloaks and scattered belts littered the ground beneath the village walls. Then there were the bodies. So many bodies.

"What is this?" She whispered. Between her and the wide-open gates was a carpet of dead.

"These are Batrun's Spears. There must be a hundred or more here." Cenos, a middle-aged woman with a sour disposition, stopped to peer down at a cluster of three staring corpses.

"How did Venza and our Spears fend off so many? Those are our people still alive in the village." Lyda pointed and then kicked her heels, urging her mount forward, surging up the trail, impatient to know the fate of her husband and son.

The faces that met her were wan and thin-lipped. Here and there a villager nodded to her in recognition. Lyda ignored them and slid from her horse to the ground when it slipped on blood slick stone a second time. She raced on foot up the hill, the cries of anguish from her fellow riders following her as they discovered the fate of their loved ones.

She slapped aside the curtain and sprang breathless into her home. Venza lay on a cot, skin clammy and mottled, a multitude of cuts on his arms and torso. A large wadding on his gut leaked pus and the air was rank with his smell.

"Venza!" She fell to her knees beside his cot and placed a hand on his cheek.

He opened his eyes with difficulty, crusted accumulations thick on the eyelashes.

"You have returned." His voice was a whisper. "Things have gone badly, Lyda. The gods have turned their backs on us."

Lyda's eyes ranged over his once muscular body, shocked at how he had wasted away. Then her heart lurched again. Dubgetious!

"My son? Does Dubgetious live, Venza?"

Tears welled and ran from his eyes. "He is taken as a levy to the Barca's army."

Lyda rocked back on her heels, a cry of despair rising from deep within her and bursting from her lips. "The Barca came here? He has taken my son?" Her hands curled into fists that she used to beat her chest and then she raked at her arms with her nails, raising welts and drawing blood. "Dubgetious! My son!" Her wail filled the small dwelling place.

Venza groaned at the sight of her anguish and tried to sit. Falling back, he began coughing and choking. Only once his face had purpled, did Lyda relent her mourning and rage. She turned him onto his side and eased his breathing, rubbing his back.

When he was able to speak, he told her of what had happened. How he and his Spears were defeated fighting the Barca alongside the Oretani. Then Batrun's promised spears arriving to confront the Barca's powerful army and being overwhelmed outside the walls before streaming away to the east. He ended by admitting to her he had encouraged Dubgetious to offer service to the Barca. How in doing so, her son had led twenty more Bastetani Spears to pledge their service.

"They would all have been killed on their knees, Lyda. The Barca is pitiless and will not rest until he has taken whatever he sets his eyes upon."

Lyda grunted as she rose, her knees popping. She found an amphora of vinegar and poured a little into a cup before filling it with water. Her movements were deliberate and focused. She sipped, nodded and knelt again beside Venza. With no expression or kind words, she held his head and allowed him to drink until he turned his face away.

Breathing heavily, he spoke with his eyes closed. "I know you will go after Dubgetious."

Lyda drank the remaining draught, saying nothing.

He opened his eyes and gazed at her. "Send me on now, Lyda. I find I wish to visit with my ancestors." He smiled, eyes cloudy with fever.

Lyda placed the empty cup on a shelf and drew her short knife, holding it in a reverse grip so the blade ran up along the inside of her arm. Kneeling beside her husband once more, she cradled his head with her left arm and touched his brow with her lips.

"Better he had died here than in service to the Barca." She growled suddenly and lifted her killing hand high. The blade flashed once and then she buried it in Venza's chest, slamming it home with such force the blade snapped at the hilt. Venza's eyes flew wide and his mouth opened as his back arced, lifting his torso from the cot. He remained like that for a heartbeat before slumping back.

Lyda stood. Stumbled, trembling. Her nostrils flared as she panted. She stared at Venza's lifeless corpse and then spat on it. She noticed that she still clutched the bone handle of her knife and hurled it at the dead man with a snarl of fury.

For two days Lyda was occupied with the task of building pyres and sending the numerous dead on to their ancestors. Two days in which she seethed with the need to recover her son. In the long hours of daylight, she toiled with axe and ox to cut trees and haul the fallen trunks to the valley. When night fell, she weighted the curtain of her home and sat in brooding silence, her thoughts filled in turn with fear, anger and despair. On the second night, just as her chin touched her chest and sleep began to curl through her mind, she started awake. Her hand sought her spear and she pulled herself to the edge of the cot, alert for the sound that had brought her to wakefulness. It came again, a scratching on the curtained doorway. She rose and in two strides was beside it.

"Who seeks me?" She hissed.

"I, the Herb Queen." A muted voice answered.

Lyda grimaced. "I did not send for you. What is it you want?"

"Vengeance." A pause. "Much the same as you."

Lyda frowned, but released the weighted curtain and drew it aside. "Come in."

"My thanks."

A shadowed figure stepped into the dark of Lyda's home and she felt for a lamp and struck a spark, igniting the oiled wick, tamping it to light the room and reveal the Herb Queen. Her eyes adjusted to the light and she eyed the woman before her. She was taller than Lyda and younger by more than a handful of years. Lyda noted that the woman's eyes were ringed by dark circles and her hair was limp. She exuded an air of despair. No, not that. Rather, a reflection of Lyda's own feeling of loss.

The Herb Queen's eyes roamed the small room, hitching at the empty cot in which Dubgetious would have been asleep, then settling on Lyda's helmet and shield.

"Drink?" Lyda lifted a jug.

The Herb Queen's eyes refocused and she shook her head.

The woman's hands were clutching her cloak tight to her bosom and Lyda intuitively knew why. Her own fatigue and turmoil fell away and she stepped forward and enfolded the young woman in her arms.

The Herb Queen's body went rigid, but after a tense heartbeat her shoulders slumped and then the woman was weeping silently onto Lyda's shoulder.

They spoke deep into the night. Owls hooted beyond the curtain, mice scrabbled through the thatch and bats shrilled under the eaves.

The Herb Queen spoke of Beratza and the love they had found together. She talked of Dubgetious too and it was plain to Lyda that the Herb Queen admired the youth and had not resented Beratza's desire to lay with him. Lyda held the Herb Queen's hand tight when she told of the battle between the Bastetani and Hamilcar Barca's warriors. Of her terror for Beratza when the gates were forced and how Beratza and Dubgetious had fought side by side every step. Tears streamed down the cheeks of both women as the Herb Queen recounted the final horrific moments of the battle when the bastard warriors of many tribes had rampaged through the village. The horrors were as vivid to Lyda as they were to the Herb Queen who had seen Dubgetious fall and Beratza's violation and death.

They drank. Lyda poured them cups of strong ale taken from the ale skin hung in a rock cistern dug into the floor of the house. It was icy and carried the scent of barley and yeast. Best of all, it numbed the pain of recollection and vivid images.

"When do you wish to go?" The Herb Queen asked, tracing the rim of her cup with a finger stained black by the herbs she worked with.

"I must speak with the warriors who rode with me. Four of them lost kin to the Barca's warriors. There are two others here who may wish to ride with us." Lyda replied at once. She had thought long about who she would ask to accompany her, never once considering the woman beside her.

"You will allow me to ride with?" The usual confidence of the woman was like a memory of a past summer.

Lyda looked deep into her dark eyes. "It would be an honour to have you ride with us." She placed a hand over the Herb Queen's own. "There is no need for you to carry a spear. Your administrations with herbs will be a great gift for I expect that before we return, there will be those of us that taste iron."

Chapter 4

Autumn cold leeched the heat from his body, turned his feet numb and throbbed through his hips and spine. His cloak was of little use as it was damp still from an earlier river crossing. A log popped in a nearby fire, but what heat it gave off was felt by others, never reaching him where he lay on the cold ground and sharp-edged rocks. His shivering would have kept him awake if not the images that pulsed in his mind. He sent a plea to Endovex to bring him peace, to banish the memories, but they remained along with the cries. He turned stiffly, trying not to release the scant warmth from under his cloak. Footsteps crunched closer and a figure loomed at his feet.

"Get your hand off your little spear and take a turn on watch." The gruff order was punctuated by a painful kick delivered to his knee.

Dubgetious jerked and hissed at the pain the kick ignited. Sitting quickly, he drew his legs up to avoid a second kick. "I have no spear." He stood.

"No need for a spear and even if there was, you would be a fool to think I would put one in your hands." The Turdetani warrior bared his teeth and laughed aloud, engulfing Dubgetious with breath that reeked of offal.

"Where?" The Bastetani youth asked.

The Turdetani pointed at a row of wagons. "Circle them until sunrise." His hand shot out, ensnaring Dubgetious by the elbow, squeezing with brute force. "If so much as a single ear of corn goes near your mouth, Bastetani, I will knock your teeth down your throat to fetch it back up." Dubgetious stood silently and the Turdetani shook his elbow, trying to draw a protest of pain from the youth. Failing to do so, he thrust Dubgetious away. "Get on with it."

Dubgetious snatched up his cloak and tossed it over his shoulders before stalking off to the wagons. The very wagons that had been loaded with produce plundered from his own village. He thought he could smell the scent of newly smoked hams, but for once he had no appetite. He had watched hams, amphorae of oil and grain sacks been taken from stony faced villagers and stacked high in the wagon beds, leaving them precious little to survive on until the following season's harvest.

He had been awake since then and the sun was high when the column halted. Dubgetious sank to his knees at the side of the track the moment word was passed down the column. Since joining the Barca's army, he had eaten nothing but a handful of over-ripe berries picked as he marched and a sliver of crust dropped by a wasteful Turdetani. Lightheaded and weary beyond measure, his eyes were closing when a Turdetani kicked him in the back. Dubgetious, wearing only his tunic, felt his skin split and fiery pain lit up his back as the hard-edged sandal struck. Snarling, he spun and caught the warrior's foot with both hands. With a furious heave, he threw the man off balance. The warrior fell and Dubgetious dropped on him, his fist raised to slam into the bastard's already crooked nose.

A hand stayed his. "There are bad ideas and worse than bad ideas, Bastetani." A tall warrior spoke, his fingers curled around Dubgetious' wrist. "Hitting that creature is well into the very worst of ideas." The warrior's face was a mere shadow, but he spoke with deep authority.

The Turdetani bucked and threw him. "I will flay your hide you worthless goat shit." The Turdetani dragged a pitted bronze blade from a mangy leather sheath.

"You will not! He is needed." The other spoke. Dubgetious tried to make out the speaker's features. "Here, you look like you are about to spew your water. Have you been fed?" Dubgetious' eyes flicked to the Turdetani glowering at him and then back at the speaker. He shook his head. "Not since we gave our service to the Barca. None of us have."

The speaker stepped towards the Turdetani. "You play a dangerous game. No doubt you are selling their provisions on. Warriors need food so be sure these people all get their allotted rations."

Suspiciously, Dubgetious watched this dark-skinned warrior, darker even than the most sunburned Bastetani. He was tall, lanky even, but Dubgetious knew such men often possessed muscles like cords of iron. The warrior turned to gaze at Dubgetious, his eyes black and close set with a large hooked nose curved over a thick, well-groomed moustache and beard.

"You are the boy that spoke Greek to the general. Do many of your people speak that tongue?"

Dubgetious shook his head. "No. I learned it from my mother."

"Well more fortune to you. How about horses? Ever ridden?" Dubgetious nodded. "Ah, the son of a leading man then. Well, we have need of messengers with an understanding of Greek. Are you willing?" Dubgetious hesitated, unprepared to be separated from his fellow Bastetani. Seeing his doubt, the warrior frowned. "You will receive a silver stater every tenday once you are accepted. More immediately though, you will sleep in a decent tent, get a new tunic and sandals and best of all, good rations."

Dubgetious' stomach lurched, reminding him of his hunger. Unsure of what new challenges he would face, but unafraid of meeting them, he rose, dusted off his filthy tunic and nodded.

"My name is Dubgetious, son of Venza. You have not told me your name."

The blow was sudden and vicious. The warrior did possess great strength and he was fast too. His cheek split across the bone and Dubgetious lurched back, eyes rolling.

"Pay attention to the way you talk to me, Bastetani." The warrior smiled coldly. "I am Berut of Sulci. Follow."

The Sulcian turned and walked on into the throngs of warriors pushing up the rutted tracks.

The Turdetani spat and gave Dubgetious a malicious leer. "You think you are getting a cosy task." His head shook as he laughed. "You will be begging to come back to our lowly ranks by sunrise."

Dubgetious shrugged and threw a vulgar gesture at the Turdetani before following Berut through the ranks of newly levied warriors. He remained silent, blood trickling unfelt from his swollen cheek, as the warrior sought out more who could converse in Greek. He was joined by three men and two women whom Berut decided held promise. All were older than him and all came from places to the south or west of which he had never heard.

As they trudged along sullenly in Berut's footsteps, Dubgetious tried to get a measure of the warriors that followed Hamilcar Barca. Since Berut concentrated his search amongst the newest arrivals, Dubgetious saw large numbers of Turdetani and many Turduli. These were warriors who had opposed Hamilcar Barca and been defeated like his own Bastetani.

Towards evening, as the column slowed and spread out to build their camp for the night, Berut led the silent company through lines of warriors that came from far shores, greeting many by name. A crowd was growing around a circle of wagons, clamouring for rations. Berut bulled his way to the tailboard of a wagon guarded by two large warriors wielding clubs and fierce expressions.

"I requisition a tent and clothing." He turned to Dubgetious and the little group of silent strangers, appraising their tattered clothing. "Six tunics, pairs of sandals and belts. Oh, cloaks and blankets too."

Dubgetious thought the warriors would send Berut off with a curse, but one of them hopped from the back of the wagon and held out a hand. Berut pulled a pouch from within his tunic and dropped two silver staters into the outstretched palm along with a lead disc etched with symbols. Dubgetious shook his head in wonder for his mother had spoken of symbols that meant words and shown him some.

Berut signalled Dubgetious forward along with another sturdy man. "Select a tent from among this lot."

Dubgetious glanced at his fellow who was eyeing him and nodded. Together they clambered onto mounds of folded tents, avoiding those with obvious damage and those that stank of rotted hide. Dubgetious pulled a goat hide tent free and rolled it over. It stank less and had fewer rips than the others he had examined. His companion looked over and shrugged.

"Best of the lot I guess."

Dubgetious jumped to the ground and his companion laid the folded tent on his broad shoulders. It weighed as much as a full-grown warrior, but Dubgetious merely grunted and shifted it to a more comfortable position.

The others had been busy collecting their new clothes and bedrolls and now Berut hustled them all closer to the centre of the camp. He halted them and turned, examining the half-erected tents nearby and the manner of men and women building them and lighting cook fires. Satisfied, he pointed a finger at Dubgetious.

"You and your new fellows will set the tent up here." He gestured to the two women. "You and you, come with me to fetch your meals. Tomorrow you will collect dry rations and prepare your own food." Berut led the two silent women off to another circle of wagons.

Dubgetious let the tent drop to the hard ground, raising a cloud of dust. He looked at the three men standing in a circle, every bit as lost as he was.

"I have slept under my cloak for four nights and I do not care how bad this thing smells, I am going to sleep well within it tonight." He grinned.

The others looked on, faces emotionless. The man that helped select the tent reached under his tunic and scratched between his legs for a moment. "I almost pity the tent, because it is about to be overrun by the hungriest bastard lice in Iberia." The others scratched in sympathy and grins spread on their dirt encrusted faces. Laughing, they began to unfurl the hide walls and count out the poles.

Their role, the Sulcian explained on the morning of their first day, was to deliver messages and orders to those who did not know either Greek or the common pidging Greco-Phoenician dialect. The veteran warriors in Hamilcar Barca's army had an easy patois that allowed them to converse despite their diverse cultures. The growing numbers of Iberian levies unable to follow orders were already the cause of friction in the camp and would cause confusion in battle.

"Of you Iberians, Hamilcar Barca, The Thunderer of Carthage, expects his orders to be delivered word for word to those that do not speak in a civilised tongue."

In the days that followed, Dubgetious and his fellows were introduced to life in the Barca army and shown what was required of them. The Sulcian remained cold and commanding, expecting them to obey him unquestioningly. As Dubgetious had quickly discovered, the warrior used his fists at the slightest offence and each of them nursed bruises and swellings. For Dubgetious' part, he was astounded by the order in the centre lines of the command, in the efficiency with which Hamilcar Barca and his leading men led the army and supplied the needs of the men and women who fought for the Barca's aims in Iberia.

The Sulcian's cold hostility never thawed, not even as they became adept at identifying Carthaginian symbols and recognising orders trumpeted across the heads of the thousands of warriors. Dubgetious learned a little more of the warrior and his origins each day. Named Berut of Sulci, he was not a Carthaginian as Dubgetious had presumed, but had been a citizen of the city of Sulci on the island of Sardinia. The names meant little to Dubgetious, but the anger he saw in Berut's face when he spoke of a faraway people who had stormed and sacked his city was frightening in intensity.

Chapter 5

The warrior feinted to her right and just as fast, came back at him off her right leg, shield held high and practice spear thrusting at his left thigh. Dubgetious twisted away and slapped his own spear down on her helmet, except she had anticipated his strike and instead, it was the rim of her shield that struck, taking him on his hip. He cursed at the pain and fell back with a gasp.

Berut laughed while the others drummed their spears against their shields. The woman, a stocky warrior of the Turdetani, grinned at Dubgetious and flicked her wrist, making an obscene gesture. He sighed and limped from the circle. A warrior of the Turduli people stepped past him with a grin, ready to prove he could defeat the Turdetani woman. Dubgetious grabbed a waterskin and upended it over his mouth, gulping down the vinegar water. He was the most powerfully built of the messengers Berut had gathered and the youngest, yet he always lost in their occasional afternoon bouts. He sat down heavily and a greasy-haired fellow leaned close, fetid breath on Dubgetious' cheek.

"You lost to her on purpose. She has you by the sack, yes?" Fingers, so called because he only had eight of his ten fingers left, sniggered good naturedly.

"I lost because… gods, I lost because she is better than me." Dubgetious slapped his helmet in frustration. "You all are!"

Fingers shoved his left hand in Dubgetious' face, displaying the maimed limb proudly. "I too lost a fight or two, but I learned. That is all you have to do."

"Well I seemed to have learned well how poor a warrior I am. It is a good thing we messengers are not required to fight."

Fingers frowned. "You just need to be better than you were the time before." He gripped Dubgetious' nose with his maimed hand and tweaked it with a jeer.

Dubgetious pushed the man's hand away. "I would prefer not to lose any body parts while I am learning." He rubbed his bruised hip and lifted his tunic to see a purple bruise spreading there.

A horseman called from a distance and trotted on towards their little group. Berut rose to meet him and Dubgetious watched for a moment before his attention was claimed by the whack of spear on shield and the grunts of the two warriors sparring.

"Watch their feet. See how they keep their balance? The first one to miss their balance will be the loser." Fingers nodded sagely.

Engrossed in the even contest, Dubgetious winced as Finger's elbowed him in the ribs, drawing his attention to their leading man and the rider.

"Something is up. Look at the bastard's face. Like a pair of virgins just lifted their tunics for him."

It was true that Berut's face was glowing with excitement. The others also noticed, even the two warriors sparring. Their blows faltered then stopped. The rider turned his mount and trotted away leaving Berut wringing the hilt of his sword. The warrior from Sulci spun around and smiled widely at them.

"Who here is of the Oretani? None? That is good." Berut clapped his hands loudly. "It is good because they wish to make war with us."

Dubgetious rubbed his bruised hip and shot a glance at Fingers. The messenger winked at him.

"Now we will put what you have learned to good use." Berut's sudden enthusiasm was replaced by a glower. "Do not fail me and if any of you worms think to sow confusion by misspeaking orders, your death will be a thing of pain."

Throughout the afternoon, Berut stormed through the camp with Dubgetious and a dwindling band of messengers in tow. He and Fingers were the last two and then Berut gestured to Fingers, beckoning him to where he was consulting with three leading men.

Fingers grunted and as he stepped away from Dubgetious' side, he muttered to the Bastetani youth. "Do what you have to pup, no more. Hear my words."

Dubgetious sidled closer to hear what was being planned. He was confident the men Fingers was being assigned to were Greek mercenaries. They were not numerous and marched in column with a band of three hundred slingers and spears of the Turduli tribe. Fingers' job would be to be sure the Iberians understood their orders and followed them.

The discussion concluded, the men parted, Fingers following the three mercenaries. He looked back at Dubgetious and mouth the words he had last spoken.

Berut frowned at Dubgetious. "Now who do I have left? Just you, young Bastetani." He looked Dubgetious up and down. "You have plenty of muscle, but for now all I require is someone who can follow orders."

Dubgetious, frustrated at being the youngest, at having to endure the condescension of the others every time he lost a bout and at being last to be placed, snapped, "I have already fought and survived a battle."

Berut's eyes hardened for just a moment before he dipped his chin. "You are right. Perhaps the worst kind of battle to survive." He offered a hard smile. "You have a fast mind and have learned well." He considered Dubgetious silently for a long moment before continuing. "You will be one of the messengers attending the General and his aides."

Dubgetious was lost in wonder. Wherever he turned, he saw men greater than the graybeards and leading men of his village and clan. Higher even than the petty kings that occasionally ruled. It had been so for the past two days, ever since Berut had taken him to the very centre of the lines, to the command compound in the midst of the Barca army. Now, a new tunic cinched tight at his waist and a pair of sandals of excellent leather, he watched from a half stade away as Hamilcar Barca strode from a large tent followed by a handful of warriors in shining armour. Hamilcar exchanged words with his sons, Hannibal and Hasdrubal, both younger than Dubgetious. Another Carthaginian, Abdmelqart laughed at Hamilcar's words and passed a remark to a surly man whose name Dubgetious failed to recall. They mounted well cared for horses and circled. Hamilcar lifted his sword and pointed it north. A drum beat began and horns blared in response.

Berut clapped a hand on Dubgetious' shoulder. "Now, mount your horse and follow."

Dubgetious followed the commanders of the great army of many tribes, his tunic setting him apart from the many others that rode and marched around him. He listened to snatched comments and watched orders been passed to veteran messengers. These too, wore tunics with the symbol of the house of Barca, a ram headed man holding aloft a sceptre. Dubgetious smoothed his tunic and fingered the design embroidered there, his thoughts returning to his people, his mother and father. To Beratza.

"You! Messenger! Are you deaf?"

Startled back to the commotion surrounding him, Dubgetious swiftly looked for the owner of the voice and found a warrior glaring at him from just paces away. The man wore chain armour and fine leather. His curled beard fell to his chest, gleaming with scented oils.

Dubgetious nodded, speechless, not knowing what message or order the man had spoken.

The warrior spat in disgust. "Find Alkmaeon the Greek. Tell him Hamilcar orders his warriors to take the right."

"Alkmaeon the Greek?"

"Here." The warrior tossed a small leather pouch to Dubgetious. "You speak the Greek tongue, yes?"

"I do." Dubgetious caught the pouch and felt the shape of a heavy disc within.

"Return to me once you have delivered the message."

Dubgetious stammered, still unable to recall who the leading man was. There had been so many strange names to remember. The warrior glowered at him. "You do not know who I am? By the gods! You are one of Berut's messengers are you not?"

"Apologies. I am newly trained."

"Curses. Win a battle with this we will not." The warrior rolled his eyes. "I am Hasdrubal."

Knowing he had failed an important test, Dubgetious tucked the message pouch inside his tunic, dreading Berut's reaction when he learned that he had forgotten the name of one of Hamilcar's leading generals.

He rode past a column of warriors who were goading one another as they pressed forward up a steep hill. Their taunts turned on him as he rode by and he urged his mount on faster. A familiar shrill trumpeting echoed over the hills as he crested the rise ahead of the warriors and pulled on the reins of his mount. Oretani warriors occupied the next hill and there were many hundreds, perhaps thousands even for more appeared with every heartbeat.

Remembering his purpose, Dubgetious wheeled his mount, seeking the Greeks and the one called Alkmaeon. He had no idea where to find him. The warriors he had passed were coming within range and a slinger sent a rock bouncing at the feet of his mount, causing it to whinny and rear back on its hind legs. Dubgetious held on grimly even as the warriors laughed and jeered him. Angry now, Dubgetious glowered at the slinger, a tall man dressed only in braccae, his chest bare.

"I am a messenger for the Barca. Do that again and your sack will find its way down your throat." Dubgetious growled.

"Ho! Big threats from a little sack with no spear!"

Dubgetious was conscious of the time wasting away and the enemy gathering at his back. "I seek the Greeks. Alkmaeon?"

The slinger looked at his fellows as they crowded closer, eyebrows raised. "Should we tell him?"

"Go on. He looks a good sort and maybe he will dip his head under your tunic."

Dubgetious turned crimson as they laughed. He gritted his teeth and was about to drive his heels into the mount's flanks when the slinger held up a hand.

"No, we jest young fellow. Alkmaeon, eh? The Greek?"

Hopeful, Dubgetious nodded.

The slinger pointed to the rear of the column. "He and his kind are back at the rear. Best hurry along with that message."

"My thanks!" Dubgetious sent his mount scrabbling down the track, furious that he had passed the Greeks somehow. He heard the laughter of the slingers at his back but paid them no heed.

He reached the bottom of the hill and a warrior stepped into his path. Dubgetious pulled hard on the reins and again his horse went up on its hind legs.

"Why do you bar a messenger's path?" Dubgetious shouted, frantic now.

The warrior shook his head and pursed his lips. "They sent you to the rear to look for the Greeks. You will not find Alkmaeon there. He and his column are marching along that tree line east of us." The warrior pointed and Dubgetious saw a column of warriors that looked very much like the Greek mercenaries.

"Then why send me to the rear?"

"You do not know what they say about the Greek's love of men?" The warrior shook his head. "Never mind. Best go before someone thinks you have stolen away on that fine mount."

"Thank you!" Dubgetious' nerves were taut as he spun his mount to the east. Racing across the face of four columns, he endured jeers and laughs from all sides. His head pounding and tears of anger in his eyes, he galloped his mount to the head of the Greek column where a knot of warriors rode.

The Greek, Alkmaeon, took the message pouch from Dubgetious and weighed it before tossing it back. "I am to take the right he says? It is good then that I was doing just that." He eyed Dubgetious and his lathered mount. "You sped here fast to tell me this. Could you not tell I was already on course?"

Dubgetious opened his mouth to answer, but no words came to him. He felt humiliated all over again. The Greek's lips twitched as though reading his thoughts and the warrior edged his mount up beside Dubgetious, leaning close to him.

"We all make mistakes. It is the lessons we learn from them that count." He turned and signalled to his column to continue, leaving Dubgetious blinking beside the marching men.

Chapter 6

The battle was short. Dubgetious, having returned to confirm to Hasdrubal that Alkmaeon had received the message, trailed after the commanders led by Hamilcar. From the crest of the hill he had ridden up earlier, the battle lines were clear and with an ear out for any new orders, Dubgetious watched the warriors close to within spear throw of the enemy. The Oretani held the higher ground and refused to surrender it as three ragged lines of Turdetani warriors advanced on their centre. Spears flew and slingers on both sides ran into the ground between the lines to hurl their slingshot at the enemy. Warriors fell sporadically and were dragged back by their kin. The Turdetani levies refused to close with the Oretani and Dubgetious heard Hamilcar's oaths from where he sat ready on his mount. Two messengers were dispatched to the flanking columns, the Greeks on the right and a force of horsemen on the left.

The Greeks marched forward, taking an easier slope toward the Oretani who began to mass on that flank. Dubgetious watched in fascination as the Greek warriors beat their spears on their shields and made steadily for the Oretani in a column twenty warriors wide and a hundred deep. Oretani spears began to fly, rising and dropping among the Greek warriors. Now the Turdetani pressed forward, encouraged by the fearlessness of the Greeks. The Oretani noticed and a hundred or more of their warriors charged the Turdetani, old enmities surfacing. Dubgetious thought the brave Oretani would quickly be cut down by the more numerous Turdetani, but was surprised at how easily they hacked their way into the Turdetani who at once faltered.

The Greeks were within strides of the Oretani, their trail littered with men speared by the numerous Oretani spears launched at them. The Oretani facing the Greeks backed up, keeping open ground between them and the now visibly labouring Greeks.

Dubgetious jumped as a hand clapped his shoulder. He turned wide eyes on Berut who frowned at him.

"See how we crush our enemies, Bastetani." Berut shoved a chin towards the warriors, his eyes glinting in the weak sun.

"You were given a message to deliver?"

"I was. By Hasdrubal." Dubgetious kept his eyes on the unfolding battle.

"The Oretani think we will cower from their few spears. They will learn in moments what a real battle is." Berut pointed off to the west.

A flutter of movement there caught Dubgetious' eye and then was gone, leaving in its wake a smudge of dust. He squinted and noticed the dust growing and in the next moment a line of horsemen crested the rise, riding hard at the Oretani's right flank. They stood rooted for a long heartbeat as the riders poured over the crest in ever-increasing numbers.

Now the Greek column, all but on its knees with exhaustion moments before, leaped forward, all pretence of exhaustion gone. Closing the gap the Oretani had carefully maintained in two bounding strides, they plunged their long spears into bare chests and shrieking faces.

With the horsemen pressing their right and the Greeks assailing their left, the Oretani lost their nerve. They broke, fleeing in groups, kin and clan racing for the higher hills at their backs and the dense tree line there.

"See there, Bastetani! Hamilcar is unstoppable!" Berut's mount skittered, sensing the excitement of its rider.

More yells and jeers sounded from around him and Dubgetious realised the other messengers, his fellow trainees, had returned. He spotted Fingers and gave him a brief nod.

Berut cursed and Dubgetious' eyes went once again to the scene being played out before them. The Oretani, lightly armed and with no heavy armour had disengaged from the Greeks and were scattering into the trees at their backs. This was by far the largest concentration of their warriors.

The horsemen had dispersed the enemy at their front and many were now hunting down fleeing groups of warriors, hurling their light spears at close range into the running Oretani. Dubgetious gasped when he saw a spear pass through a warrior's back to emerge an arm's length from his chest. The warrior crumpled in a heap of flailing limbs. The same horseman had another spear in the air less than a heartbeat later, taking another warrior through the neck. Dubgetious' mouth remained open, awed at the horseman's speed and accuracy with the spears that were barely longer than an arrow.

He blurted the question that formed in his mind. "Who are those riders?"

Berut spat. "Masulians. When they are not fighting Carthage, they are taking its silver to fight its enemies."

The hillside the Oretani had occupied was now just a pall of dust from this distance and little could be seen of the fighting, but the Oretani were no longer a threat. Already horns were sounding to gather Hamilcar Barca's army. Another victory to the Carthaginian. Dubgetious shook his head in wonder and thought of Batrun's folly in trying to stand against such a formidable force as this one. Was there a single tribe that could prevail against such numbers and skill? No, thought Dubgetious. Impossible.

Hamilcar Barca ordered the army to march north that very afternoon, surprising Dubgetious once again. Victories should be celebrated. Ale drunk, beasts slaughtered and roasted. Men and women should dance and couple. At the very least, the fallen should be sent to their ancestors on pyres and the wounded given time to rest and recover or die so that their shades could travel through Saur's lands. He was helping his companions dismantle their tent and load a wagon with their provisions. A deep groan from the far side of the wagon stopped them where they stood. Fingers put a finger to his lips and quickly leaped onto the wagon. His jaw fell as he stared at what lay on that side.

"By the gods. What are you doing? Get him to a healer!" Fingers shouted.

Dubgetious sprang around the tail of the wagon and stopped short. Two blood besmeared warriors were dragging a third between them. Dubgetious had seen the horrors caused by blades wielded in battle, but the sight of the bare-chested warrior hanging limply between his two kin shocked him into silence. The warrior's torso was flayed wide open, ribs gleaming white amidst pink sinewy flesh.

The stricken warrior chose that moment to lift his chin, eyes bright with pain and the knowledge of impending death. The slinger that had made a fool of him locked eyes with Dubgetious. The Bastetani youth lifted a hand and made a gesture to Endovex to guard this man's shade across the land of death to which he was surely going soon.

"There are no healers you goat-turd!" One of the dying warrior's kin snarled.

Fingers scrambled off the wagon, his face flushed. "Then end his agony."

"What is it to you? Get out of our way."

Fingers stared in horror at the ruin of the slinger's body and stepped hastily aside, allowing the men to proceed.

"Find your Greek, young messenger?" The slinger slurred as he passed and his eyes fixed on Dubgetious, a crooked, pain-wracked smile on his face.

Dubgetious dipped his head in respect. If he were ever so injured, he hoped that he too could show such courage.

The companions followed their wagon on their newly granted mounts. None uttered a word as they crossed the killing ground, passing first the bodies of the Greek and Turdetani warriors and then the thick tumble of Oretani corpses. There were figures sliding between the dead, shrouded and furtive even in the harsh afternoon glare. Small blades glinted in their hands as they worked and Dubgetious shivered when he heard a plea for mercy from a fallen warrior cut short by the scavenger's blade.

"Scum!" Fingers spat and fidgeted at his belt for the blade he would have carried if he were permitted.

"Where do they come from?" Dubgetious asked.

Fingers stared at him for a moment, surprise on his face.

"Where do they... they are our camp followers."

The Turdetani messenger woman who had bested Dubgetious in training rode up beside him and grinned humorously at him. "Good reason not to taste iron."

Dubgetious vision of war was changing with every step he took in Hamilcar Barca's footsteps.

Berut signalled to Dubgetious from up the column and the Bastetani kicked his mount into a canter, glad to flee the shades that lurked in that place.

The Sulci warrior's glare was filled with malice and Dubgetious guessed Hasdrubal had spoken of his ignorance. He drew up beside the warrior, teeth gritted with apprehension. There was no telling what punishment he might receive, but it would be harsh, he was certain.

"You are to ride to a Turduli village north west of here and deliver a message to Eshmun, the Carthaginian commander there." Berut shoved the familiar message pouch into his hands. His voice lowered to a lethal hiss. "You failed me today and I will not forget that. Fail to deliver this message and I will have the skin whipped from your back."

Dubgetious swallowed, his mouth dry, and took the pouch.

"I do not know the country here. Does this village have a name?"

Berut gestured with his chin at two riders walking their mounts nearby. "They know the road. Follow them and do not be delayed."

Dubgetious looked at the riders that were to accompany him. They were Masulians, the riders from Africa so skilled with their throwing spears.

"You should reach Eshmun by sundown tomorrow." The warrior whistled and the Masulian riders glanced over their shoulders at him. He rattled off orders in a tongue that was incomprehensible to Dubgetious and then with a final piercing stare at him, turned away.

The Masulians turned their mounts and circled him, their expressions hidden behind the linen that covered their faces and heads, leaving only their eyes visible.

Cold fingers traced up Dubgetious' spine and he wondered if Berut had ordered these two to kill him. He hefted the message pouch in his hand and dismissed the idea. If he had wanted Dubgetious dead, he could just as easily have killed him in front of Hamilcar. Dubgetious had no illusions about his value in this army.

He breathed deeply. "Greetings!"

The Masulians wheeled their ponies and trotted away.

Dubgetious urged his mount after them. It was a good deal taller than theirs and no doubt better suited to a long ride through hills and valleys. There was no fear of losing them, on the contrary, if the message was so cursed important, why not give him scouts with sturdier mounts?

With the column long distant, Dubgetious began to suspect sorcery. He pushed his mount hard in the wake of dust left by the pair of Masulians, but no matter how hard he did, they remained ahead of him. The insides of his knees chaffed, his buttocks ached, and cramps threatened to spasm in his thighs. He had a single waterskin, and that was already half empty. Although late in the year, the heat was still intense, sapping up his strength.

The Masulians pulled further ahead and he feared they were leading him into the wilderness to be found and gutted by some aggrieved tribesman. The gods alone knew there were many of them in this land. He glanced at his light-coloured tunic, bright in the lowering sun and the red stitching of the Barca crest glowing bloody. Any keen-eyed warrior watching from the hills around would know him for what he was at once. He pressed his mount with renewed urgency to close on the pair of scouts who had disappeared into broken, hilly country.

Following their path into the tree line, tall trees swayed above and he found himself on a narrow path alongside a gorge. Water splashed out of sight beneath the growth that hid the stream. His horse whinnied, and he focused on the path, trying to see into the growing gloom ahead. Movement on his right nearly sent him screaming from his mount's back and into the gorge. Holding back his terror, he squinted into the shadows and saw one of the Masulians pacing him.

"Where the curses did you go?" Dubgetious wanted to bellow at the rider, but kept his voice to a hiss, afraid that a shout would echo far down the gorge and alert enemy warriors.

The Masulian eyed him for a heartbeat and then gestured to him to follow. The man turned his mount uphill and disappeared within a stride. Dubgetious gaped. How did he do that? Heart pounding, he spat and made a gesture to Endovex to guard his shade from malicious spirits, certain these two were possessed. He turned his horse and leaned low to avoid the branches that hung over the narrow path left by mouflon and deer. Rounding a large tree, he wiped his face, trying desperately to rid his eyelids of a spiderweb that had brushed over him. His mount stopped and he almost toppled from its back in surprise. Cursing furiously under his breath, he saw the reason. The two Masulians were stretched out on their cloaks at the base of a large lichen-covered boulder. They eyed him in silent disdain before laying back on the cloaks and closing their eyes.

Dubgetious glared at them, but pressed his lips together and resolved to ride harder the following day. He slid from his mount and despite his best efforts at silence, he grunted in pain when his feet touched the ground and both legs cramped. He glared at the Masulians, certain he had heard a smothered laugh.

Chapter 7

The path of the army was not difficult to follow. While there were many lesser trails made by small columns of warriors scouting or foraging, the trail left by the core of the Barca army had scarred the land. The ground was rutted by numerous wagon wheels, the banks of streams had been churned muddy and whole groves of trees had been felled.

"They have their heart set on someplace in the north." Tascux grunted, pointing with his chin to where the trail crossed a saddle in a range of hills that ran roughly east to west. He ran his fingers through his greased beard, catching a louse and cracking it between his teeth. He was a warrior with many seasons at his back and had often raided Oretani settlements far into the north.

Lyda rinsed her mouth with a draught from her waterskin, savouring the tart strength of the watered vinegar.

"The hills mark the land of the Oretani which you know well. What draws them that way?" She asked him for she had never ridden north.

"Some few towns and villages. Perhaps even Castulo." The Bastetani warrior looked over his shoulder, marking the progress of the four riders accompanying them. "The Herb Queen slows us." He took the opportunity to slide from his mount and let loose a stream of urine beside the path.

"She has suffered as have we both. Us all." Lyda responded, flexing her back to release the kinks that settled in her muscles more easily as she aged. She wondered if the Barca would dare to strike for Castulo. It was the Oretani's chief city and Lyda knew with certainty that the Oretani would fight hard to keep it.

Tascux wiped his hands on his tunic. "I am ready for death and more than ready to kill the Barca's Spears, but what will she do?"

Lyda shook her head. "Runeovex will find a use for her. You know of the Oretani leading man, Orissus. Can this Barca army overcome him?"

For the first time in the two days they had been following the Barca army, Tascux face showed a trace of the emotions hidden within.

"You know my wife was Oretani?" Lyda nodded. "You know how I came to be the lucky bastard she chose?"

She gritted her teeth. Tascux had found his wife's body among the dead. Her death had been a hard one, her head having been hacked from her shoulders with a blunted blade.

"Twelve of us stood outside her village gates shaking our spears, hungry for their bounty. Four times a champion from among their warriors came out to fight one of ours. The fourth was a beast. A giant seeded by Orco, god of rock and mountain himself." Tascux lifted himself onto his mount's back. "We drew lots and it was my fortune that put me chest to chest with this giant. I was so afraid I could not decide if I should shit or piss myself." His eyes grew pale. "So, I set my spear and cursed his kin and clan."

"You slew him of course?" Lyda's patience was thin, but she knew this could be the only time the old warrior would tell this tale.

"For all his size, he was hairless. Not a hair. Bald, no beard, not even eyebrows. Can you believe that?" Tascux shook his head. "He thrust his spear faster than an adder strikes, but I was faster still. We circled and tried to blood our blades in one another but were too well matched. He tried to anger me with curses. I tried getting the sun in his eyes. Nothing made any difference." He took a draught and gauged the distance of the other four riders. "We fought like that while the shadows shortened, and the sun grew fierce above us. The Oretani were jeering us from their walls and my companions were cursing me. You know how I killed him?"

"The sun addled his mind and you gutted him?"
Tascux pursed his lips. "I asked him which mother hen shat out the egg that was his head." He slapped his thigh, sending flies buzzing. "Their great champion lost his mind alright. He went purple with rage and charged me. Tripped on a frayed sandal strap and I put my spear in his eye faster than shit sinks."

"And you won your wife?"
He gave Lyda a puzzled look. "The bald warrior was my wife's promised. She sprang from the wall and took up his blade. I was still trying to pull my spear out of his eye." He lifted his hands from his lap and turned them palm up. "I had to hold her off with just my hands. Even so, she nearly had my throat with her teeth." He nodded as the other riders closed.

"It was a grand spectacle and two of my companions used it to steal over their walls and take the best of the Oretani mounts out the back gate. The Oretani went berserk and blamed the girl even as she was struggling to kill me."

Lyda's chin dipped. "Your tale has power. It is well that you have held it close all these seasons." Lyda turned the words in her mind. How could she battle a giant and win her son?

The following day, they reached the hills and saw a sight that stopped them short. Their ascent into the hills on the Barca army's trail had warmed them after a shivering night wrapped in cloaks and huddled around a small fire. Now they felt a cold more chilling than any winter night at the sight that screamed at them in silent blood.

"So many." Cenos, a warrior woman of middling years muttered.

The rest stared, appalled at the number of dead left to be feasted upon by the multitudes of carrion birds. Of them, only Lyda and Tascux remained unmoved.

Outrage growing, Cenos cursed. "Why did they not send them on their way to the ancestors?"

Lyda clicked her tongue and her mount began the descent.

"The Barca cares not for the lives of the warriors, only on capturing his next prize."

"We should gather villagers and build pyres or the shades of these dead will never cross Saur's domain." Cenos' voice rose.

Lyda saw where the Oretani had fallen while facing the enemy and the scattered corpses of the enemy that had attacked up the hill. She turned to track the flight of the Oretani warriors by the bodies that stretched to the woods overlooking the battleground. The dead were numerous, too numerous even for the carrion birds to consume and many had bloated and turned a foul blackened colour.

A breeze lifted, blowing from the north and the stench of death made their eyes water and guts heave. They spat to ward off the shades of these dead warriors and tucked their faces beneath their tunics to escape the stench and flies.

Tascux kicked his mount forward and turned east, passing Lyda without a word. The others paused at her side, unsure whom to follow.

"He rides upwind to escape the stink." The Herb Queen spoke, showing no concern for the smell.

Lyda nodded and set off with the others after Tascux. Crossing the right of the battleground, they passed among the fallen Greek mercenaries and the Oretani that had faced them before they escaped the stink of corruption.

Skirting the great swath of dead, they carried on to the tree line and regained the trail of Hamilcar Barca's army. Cenos looked back and her cry alerted the others whose spears were raised even as they whirled their mounts to face the pounding hooves that raced towards them. Two score riders on ponies were hurtling from the western edge of the battlefield.

"There are too many to fight!" Lyda yelled, turning her mount away.

They fled into the trees, hanging low over their mounts' withers to avoid whipping branches, seeking the fastest routes through the trees and thick undergrowth. Crossing a stony watercourse, dry at this time of the year, they raced up a slope before veering north to avoid an impenetrable wall of thorn. Behind them rose spine chilling ululations foreign to the land.

"By the gods, there is no way through that!" Audoti snarled.

"Keep riding. We have a good lead." Lyda encouraged him and the others. "There!" She spotted a break in the thorns and rode through it, finding herself nearing the top of a small hill whose reverse slope was steep and rocky. Lyda heard the enemy in front of them before she saw them.

"What in Orco's name is that sound?" Cenos cried.

They all listened to the unearthly trumpeting, eyes wide.

Tascux brandished his spear and pointed. "There walks a demon."

Lyda blinked in disbelief. Creatures the size of boulders were stalking the trail that crossed before them. Gray in colour, with large ears that fanned out alongside their heads from which extended a snake-like arm and a pair of blade length tusks, they were a horror to behold. Then she saw the single rider seated upon the neck of each beast and she knew what they were.

"They are not demons, but a creature of war from a far land." Lyda called to the others who were backing their horses up, ready to face the overwhelming number of riders at their backs rather than demons such as these.

Tascux glared down the hill. "They have seen us." He looked at Lyda. "Can they be killed?"

She nodded, uncertainly. "Not by us and not today. Now we run."

Again, they urged their horses east while behind them enemy riders followed, seeking to blood themselves on the small band. The wind whipped at their faces, growing stronger with each passing moment, heralding a coming storm, the first of the autumn. A flash of fire streaked through the sky followed three heartbeats later by a crash of thunder. The gods were watching. They veered further east and Tascux edged past Lyda.

"I know this land! There is a good place to lose these bastards ahead, but we must be out of their sight to do so!"

Lyda nodded and felt the first spit of rain sting her cheek. She glanced over her shoulder at her companions. The Herb Queen had fallen behind by five or more lengths and was clearly struggling to remain astride her mount. She cursed and pulled her mount around, allowing Cenos, Eppa and Audoti to pass her. She caught the Herb Queen's mount by its bridle and hauled her mount close, pulling both to a halt.

"What are you doing?" A thunderclap almost drowned out the Herb Queen's words.

"Saving you!" Lyda swung from her mount up behind the Herb Queen and grabbed the reins from her. Savagely, she dug her heels into the animal's flanks and started it forward under a rising gale as the storm closed on them.

Tascux was waiting ahead, his mount lathered and tossing its head at every crack of thunder.

"Up there! Go!" He pointed up a steep path that snaked its way to the top of a flat-topped hill.

Lyda gritted her teeth and clenched her knees to hold her seat, instructing the Herb Queen to do likewise. The rain was falling harder and she knew the steep path would soon be impossible to ride. Already the mount was having to claw and scrabble for grip on the wet surface.

Only when she reached the top, rain streaming from her hair and down her tunic, running in torrents beneath the hooves of the mount, did she look back. The sun still shone from the west, painting the scene beneath her in vivid relief against the backdrop of storm clouds.

Tascux had dismounted and sent his mount up the slope. He had remained a third of the way up, perched on a flat rock, like a lynx prepared to fall on his prey. That prey was now coming. Of the two score riders that had pursued them, only three had been close enough to see them cut back up this goat path. None had remained to signal the route to their companions.

The enemy riders' mounts seemed to have no difficulty climbing the steep path and very soon the first rider came up alongside the ledge on which Tascux waited, spear poised.

Even as thunder boomed above and around them, the Bastetani warrior plunged his spear into the man's shoulder directly beneath his ear. The spearhead, sparkling in the sunlight disappeared into the man and then emerged, drawing a spray of blood with it. Tascux spun on the ball of his left foot and hurled the heavy spear at the third of the enemy riders. Lyda heard the impact of the spear from her position on the hill, a deep hollow thwack that tumbled the warrior from his mount with no cry ever rising to his lips.

The surviving rider screamed a war cry that was drowned out by the hammering of the gods above and then he was hurling his own spear.

Tascux was already airborne, his short knife raised. He dropped on the remaining warrior and both flew from sight into the thick brush beside the track.

Cenos gasped and Audoti, the remaining male warrior in Lyda's little company, cursed and slipped from his mount.

"Hold!" Lyda barked.

Audoti spat. "He may still live!"

"He may, but if you charge down there, the enemy will see you." She gestured with her chin to where the remaining enemy riders now appeared, casting fruitlessly for signs of their passage in the muddied ground. The rain had washed away their tracks, but there were three riderless ponies strung out along the goat path. At any moment one of the riders might notice them or the ponies could retreat down the hillside and then the enemy would know where to hunt for them.

Chapter 8

"We should ride now." Hissed Cenos, although there was little chance of her voice carrying above the wind and thunderclaps.

Lyda was torn. Cenos was right and the enemy's riderless mounts had seen the riders below. The pony furthest down the steep path turned in an agitated circle, spraying brilliant plumes of rain from its shaggy mane. Audoti's hope that Tascux had survived the leap onto the last enemy rider and the fall down the steep slope was slight, but Lyda also held that hope. Tascux may well be alive and if he was, he would surely be injured. They had a Herb Queen who could save him. Unless they fled.

"We will wait." She spoke, her voice firm. She slid from the Herb Queen's mount and regained her own horse's trailing reins, passing them to the Herb Queen.

Cenos spat and turned her mount away while Audoti nodded in approval. Lyda respected the tall, lean warrior almost as much as Tascux.

"Audoti, if the enemy come up the slope, can we hold them?" The warrior's lip lifted at the corner in a sneer. "They would need to have wings to come off that path and at us. We can hold."

"How long do we wait?" The Herb Queen asked.

"Until nightfall if we have to. We will search for Tascux then and pray to Runeovex in the meantime to keep watch over his spear follower." She glanced to where Cenos was hobbling her mount in the lee of a jagged rock. "Take the mounts to Cenos." Eppa sprang from her mount and passed the reins to the Herb Queen along with those of Audoti's horse.

The warrior woman carried her spear and a short sword was sheathed under her right arm. She was almost as tall as Audoti and had broad shoulders, capable of holding her own when wrestling her companions during celebrations. The woman was there because her young son had been killed during the attack on their village, ridden down in the narrow alleys into which he had fled. Her husband had crossed the land of Saur two summers earlier. She crept to the lip of the rise and peered down from behind the cover of thick brush.

"They have left three of their number at the foot of the trail." She turned to Lyda and Audoti. "They will see the ponies."
Lyda crept up between Audoti and Eppa, laying on the wet rock and icy mud. The ponies were making their way down the trail and in just a few more paces would clear a large, bushy tree, the only reason they had not yet been seen.

A movement beside the path caused the lead pony to lean back on its haunches. The three watchers held their breath as an arm snaked out of the foliage and into view. A pause, and then a helmet appeared. The enemy wore cloth on their heads, but this was not Tascux' helmet they saw. Instead, as the man turned to look up the track, they saw an unfamiliar hairless face. The man pulled himself onto the path, head swinging from the enemy below to the skittish ponies. He slowly rose to his knees and then his feet, one hand outstretched to the mounts.

"Who is he?" Audoti whispered.

"Not Bastetani, but perhaps not of the enemy either." Lyda observed, then her eyes widened as the unknown warrior laid a hand on the muzzle of the closest pony. Moments later, he was at its neck and then he had a hand in the horse's ragged mane. Slowly he turned it uphill and began to climb.

"He has the ear of the horses." Audoti sighed with respect.

"There are more with him." Lyda noticed several more helmets shifting through the chest high summer grass and thorn.

The trio watched as the warrior led the pony up the path. The two remaining ponies turned and followed. Behind them slunk the handful of hidden warriors.

Lyda was crouched, spear ready at the head of the steep goat track when the warrior stepped off the path and onto the flat ground at the summit of the hill, hand still buried in the mount's mane.

Before she could rise, he silenced her with a gesture. "Move back. Move back. I have her, but she is still jumpy from the storm."

Lyda started at his speech. Audoti noticed and pulled her back without any sudden motions. Eppa too, stepped back, her spear levelled.

The warrior noticed and smiled, teeth white against his dark skin. "You can put your spears away, Bastetani. We are no enemies of yours."

The two remaining ponies appeared, paused to scent the strangers and nickered softly before following their leader.

"There we go." The warrior released the mount and tossed a handful of nuts towards the Bastetani horses. The ponies followed, scrubbing them up from the mud as they went. More warriors emerged from the trail, slinking over the rim and congregating out of sight of the enemy below.

"Greetings, Bastetani. I am Chalcon from Sucro."

Lyda's jaw dropped, astonishment writ large in her eyes.

"From Sucro?"

Chalcon grinned and nodded. "Yes. As you see from my daring and courage, everything you have heard of the warriors of Sucro is true." His grin turned cheeky.

There was a heartbeat of silence and then Audoti gave a bark of amused laughter. The others smiled and laughed too, all except Lyda.

"I too was once from Sucro." She said softly.

Chalcon's eyebrows rose to meet the rim of his helmet.

"Truly! Then the gods have had a hand in our meeting here today." He stepped forward and before Lyda could react, enfolded her in his wiry arms. "Greetings, sister of Sucro." He released her and smiled. "I may know your family."

Lyda's lips parted and then closed, her face growing cool. Instead, she pointed down the goat track. "One of our warriors lays untended down there. We do not know if he lives or if his shade has flown. Did you chance upon him?"

Chalcon's expression turned from confusion to concern.

"Not I." He looked at the warriors with him who shook their heads.

Audoti grunted and Lyda's shoulders drooped with disappointment. "We must wait until the enemy leave or night falls then."

They gathered in a wary circle, the Bastetani warriors and the warriors of Sucro. Drawing their cloaks tighter as the wind whistled through the rocks and lifted their hair. The rain ceased as the thunderstorm drifted south on the cold north wind. The season of warmth was fleeing and soon winter's cold grip would close on the land.

"It will be a cold night." Chalcon moaned. Then he grinned.

"Meeting a warrior from Sucro is a good remedy though. Tell me what brings you to the Oretani lands? Raiding?" His eyes were on Lyda.

Cenos, who had joined the circle along with the Herb Queen, spat. "Blood debts! Many of them!"

Chalcon eyed the dour warrior. "Oh? Then you will need to wait your turn I fear."

Lyda frowned. "You are here to collect blood debts?"

Chalcon chuckled. "Not I, Sister. Them." He gestured sharply over his shoulder towards the track below. "The Thunderbolt of Carthage. Hamilcar. He seeks to shackle the Oretani."

"We know this and our fight is not with the Oretani, but with this Thunderbolt." Lyda's voice was as hard and cold as the rocks they crouched on. "He sacked my home village and levied the strongest to fight in his masses. We would free them."

The warriors with Chalcon shifted and his eyes narrowed.

"The Bastetani are at war with Hamilcar Barca? This is good news!"

"How so? What is our war to you from far away Sucro?" Audoti snapped.

Chalcon waved an arm to the east. "Not so far away. We mistrust this Carthaginian. He has taken the south lands of the Turdetani and Turdeli. His greed for the silver mined from their hills has grown. In Sucro, we fear that he will not stop until he has driven us all into the Inland Sea."

"This is why you are here? You do not take Barca's silver to wield his spears?" Lyda's voice grew hopeful.

"My companions and I wished to see this Hamilcar and gauge how strong the resolve is among the people of Iberia to resist him." He paused and grimaced. "My apologies. I was thoughtless of your own suffering." His eyes locked on Lyda's.

"The people Hamilcar killed and took, they were kin?"

The Bastetani remained silent, their faces sombre. Chalcon shook his head. "As I feared. I travel far and wide and have met Bastetani of the western hills. Perhaps even those that have been taken?"

"My son." Lyda's voice cracked even as she fought to keep it steady. "Dubgetious."

Chalcon's expression clouded for just a fleeting moment, but Lyda noticed and her jaws tightened, muscles bunching in her shoulders.

"You know this name?" She whispered.

Chalcon glanced at her as though he had forgotten her presence and then shrugged noncommittally.

"The name is unusual. I thought I had heard it said before, but…" He snapped his fingers. "Too much wine I fear."

Lyda gazed at him sceptically. "Just so." She looked west towards the sun settling on those dark hills there. "It is almost nightfall. Herb Queen, prepare to tend Tascux."

The Herb Queen lifted her face and nodded to Lyda. "I have thought of the injuries he most likely suffers and am prepared." Chalcon's eyes were drawn to her face and all could see his recognition of her.

"You know our Herb Queen! Then you know my son?" Lyda's voice was sharp.

Chalcon appeared flustered. "I must do. I cannot recall the boy, but your Herb Queen tended my hand after I burned it." He nodded at her and lifted his right hand, palm out so all could see the white and pink of wrinkled scars.

The Herb Queen smiled. "Too much wine."

Chalcon laughed. "Indeed!

Audoti growled and edged to the lip of ground overlooking the trail below. A moment later he signalled to Lyda. The others joined him.

"The enemy are gone. There is still time to search for Tuscox before nightfall." Lyda stood. "Bring your medicines and bandages, Herb Queen."

She scrambled down the slope, wary of the treacherous footing. The others followed her, all making for the place they had seen Tuscox fall.

Chalcon caught up with Lyda in a few paces, uncaring of the slippery mud, springing from rock to boulder lithely.

"How will you find your people among the enemy hordes?"

She gave him an irritated look. "The gods will offer me an answer at the right time."

Chalcon knelt beside a clump of crushed bush and ran his hands over the cold body of a rider, removing a pouch from under the dead man's tunic. He hefted it and made a face.

"Before Hamilcar can march to Castulo, he must take a settlement a day's ride north and its walls are formidable." He slid the pouch under his tunic. "This will offer you a chance to find your people."

"How do you know this?" Lyda eyed the second fallen rider. Tascux had done well.

Audoti and Cenos pushed down the slope, passing her. The sun was merging into the dark hills to the west and the light was fading fast, but Lyda held Chalcon's eye.

The warrior from Sucro grinned. "Hamilcar killed many Oretani in a battle just days ago, but many more have filled this settlement I speak of. Would you leave so many enemy at your back?"

Lyda grunted, his argument sound. "And you? Are you returning to Sucro?"

Chalcon shook his head. "I must convince Orissus to raise his Spears and bring all his warriors to the fight." He spat. "His Spears would have doubled the Oretani numbers in the last battle, but at the last he refused to march."

"Yet you still hope to persuade him to fight? What is the point? Hamilcar is sure to take the fight to him."

A cry from the gloom below them drew their attention. Chalcon left her and went slipping on hands and feet like a scuttling beetle down the slope. The Herb Queen caught Lyda's arm before she too could follow the sound of the cry.

"Is he the father of your son?" The Herb Queen's eyes were wary, but there was a deeper pulse there of something akin to sympathy.

Lyda pursed her lips, fighting down her anger. "Have you always known?"

"That Venza was not Dubgetious' true father? For some few seasons." She hoisted her bag of herbs. "He knows who the father is though?"

Lyda considered. "He is that man's brother. I expect he knows."

Chapter 9

The call of a jay echoing in his ears, Dubgetious groaned. He lay face down in the leaves and dirt, a stone pressing coldly into his cheek. The jay called again and he came awake, noticing at once the usual noise of the army was absent. Sitting up, he stifled a curse at the ache in his legs, his eyes widening as he remembered where he was and the message he was to deliver. He darted a hand under his tunic and felt the familiar shape of the message pouch. He rose to his knees, his cloak falling from his body, and his heart stuttered. The Masulians were gone as were the mounts. All three horses.

Standing, he turned slowly. There was no sign of the scouts or the horses. He was in a thick forest on a hill far from home with no idea how to find the army of Eshmun. Returning to Berut without having delivered the message to Eshmun was inconceivable.

He bellowed angrily into the boughs of the trees swaying unconcerned over his head. The echoes of his despair faded and bird calls filled the silence followed by the alarmed bark of a deer. Dubgetious lifted his cloak and spear. His waterskin was empty, but he recalled there was a good stream nearby. He would find Eshmun and deliver the message. This might be a test set by Berut or the Masulians may just have decided to leave him behind. He could not say, but he would show them how resourceful a Bastetani could be.

At the stream, he drank and then filled his waterskin. The water was icy and the forms of fish lurking at the bottom of the pools could be seen. He tried to spear them, but gave up after overbalancing on a slick rock and almost falling in.

Using the sun and resuming the journey in the direction they had travelled the previous day, Dubgetious followed the trail beside the stream until it veered sharply north. He scrambled up a hillside from which he could see a great distance north. He searched in vain for any telltale signs of a village or encampment. There were none, but he spotted what appeared to be a wider trail to the west. It might lead to the village he sought. If not, it was possible he would meet travellers who could direct him. There was also the chance he would encounter warriors keen to gut anyone in Hamilcar's army.

Before he reached the trail, he began to feel the weight of eyes on his neck. He slipped between trees and kept to the shadows as he stared back the way he had come. There was no sign of watchers. He was sweating freely, his legs tingling as he pushed his pace. The leather of his sturdy new sandals was beginning to bite at the skin around his ankles and his stomach protested the lack of food. He rounded a thick stand of thorn bush and paused to tighten his belt and squash the hunger pangs. The way ahead was too steep to walk and he turned to find a better path over the hill. He had taken just two steps back when he saw the glint of sunlight reflected from a blade. The dazzling brightness was gone in a heartbeat. Dubgetious sank to his knees, his body tight against the shadowy side of a wide tree trunk. Breathing quietly, he took his time to examine the clusters of bush and deeper shadows beneath the trees. For long moments, he watched. If not for the reflection he had seen, he would have turned away. Instead, he began to use his eyes like the old hunters had spoken of and concentrated on what he saw from the sides of his vision. It was difficult and his eyes soon ached. Then, about to resume his journey, he spotted a figure. Looking directly at the figure beyond a thicket, Dubgetious could make out little, but when looking from the corner of his eye, he saw the unmistakable shape of a head and shoulder. He saw two others soon after. They were watching the ground above the thorn thicket he had stepped behind earlier, expecting him to appear there. Hunting him.

Dubgetious shuddered. These were hill warriors. The men and women who lived in the wild lands between tribes. They owned little and moved often, hunting their meals where they could and stealing and killing when the opportunity arose. Such people were often deformed and carried puss filled sores. It was said that the shades of people cursed by the gods would fill these people so they might have more than one shade within them. Dubgetious had seen two a season earlier when his father's spears had hunted them down. They had attacked a young couple just beyond the town walls, killing them gruesomely. When cornered they had fought like Saur's dogs, snarling and mad with bloodlust.

Dubgetious sank lower and edged deeper into the trees, his face averted lest they spy the sheen of sweat on his brow and cheeks. Crawling out of their sight, he shuddered and then ran, cushioning his footfalls on pine needles, slowing when he had to pass through low bush and stopping to skirt two crows fighting over the remains of a lynx kill.

He ran harder once beyond that hillside, stretching his stride to eat the ground. He kept to the shade where he could and until he saw an open expanse of ground before the trees began again. To reach the trail, he would need to cross it in full view of any watchers on the hill behind him. If they saw him from the hill, they would have a long distance to make up and he was not planning on taking a rest before he was at the gates of the village and kneeling at the feet of the Carthaginian, Eshmun.

He lowered his head and ran hard, breaking out of the tree line and parting the tall dry grass like a scythe. Ten strides into the field, he heard an exclamation of surprise and then the bone chilling sound of a bowstring released.

An arrow whipped past his head close enough that he could follow the fletching as it flew. He began to dodge from side to side like a hare before the hounds. Arms pumping, he thrust out his chest and sprinted. Whistles and claps sounded in his wake. There seemed to be many more pursuers than just the three he had spotted.

Fear lent him speed and he was well past the middle of the field when the next arrow whistled past him, followed by a third that fell from above him. He knew then that they were at the very limit of their range. If he could maintain that distance, he knew he could outrun them. Gritting his teeth, he pressed on, quickly reaching the trees and leaping a gully to land on the hard-pressed dirt of a wide track. Choosing to follow it north, he began running in a measured stride that would lap up long distances without exhausting him. His heart leaped as he recognised the deep ruts in the track. Wagons had passed this way. Very likely the road would lead to the village he sought.

A new sound reached him and a cold sweat that had nothing to do with his exertions bathed him. The rapid drumming of horses riding hard resonated up the hill. The hill warriors rarely had mounts; they tended to ride them too hard with no care and so ended up eating them once they were injured beyond use. He increased his pace, fixing his eyes on the crest of the hill and the tall trees that shadowed the track there. He had run perhaps a quarter of the distance when he sensed the horse riders come into sight of him. Unable to restrain the urge, he glanced over his shoulder and at once lost his footing on the rutted ground. He thrust his spear away from his body as he tumbled forward to avoid gutting himself and then he hit the ground, slamming into it with a knee and elbow. Pain bloomed and his breath expelled in a grunt. He was rolling to his feet the moment he fell, ignoring the scraped and bruised limbs, lifting his spear before him to point back at the riders. For one surprised heartbeat he dared to hope he was saved. The riders were the pair of Masulian scouts.

Their expressions were hidden, but their eyes were deep wells of cold unfeeling. Staring into those merciless eyes, he knew for a certainty that Berut wanted him dead. His courage began to buckle.

They slowed their mounts and lifted throwing spears to shoulder height. Dubgetious had no shield and was on his haunches in the middle of the track. Lips dry and tongue thick in his throat, he fought the urge to turn and flee. He was Bastetani and he would face his death like a champion. He heard Beratza's laughter and felt her breath on his neck. The weight of his father's eyes on him from across the bowed heads of his people. His mother and her long seasons of hidden sadness. These all came unbidden to his mind as the Masulians drew back their throwing arms.

Dubgetious sprang forward although the Masulians were twenty paces from him. He would not die huddled like a child. With a shrilled war cry emulating his father's, he threw his whole strength into casting the heavy spear.

Chapter 10

The sun cast no shadows nor was there a breeze. About him all the land turned still and shrunk from his vision. All except the Masulian at which he had aimed. The throw was good. The spear flew neatly from his hand, the bright gleam of the spearhead trailed by its spinning shaft lifted a head above the Masulian's face.

Dubgetious saw the Masulians release their spears. He knew how accurate they were and his muscles stiffened in anticipation of the pain. His ankle twisted on the rutted surface of the road, toppling him to the left. Even so, one of the thrown spears found its mark. Or almost did. It skimmed off the surface of the round iron helmet that he wore. The blow knocked his head back as he fell.

Ears ringing and lights blinking behind his eyes, he breathed in a stifling breath of dust. He clawed the ground with his hands and kicked with his feet, trying desperately to raise himself. The pounding of hoofbeats receded and in their place came the ragged crunch of footfalls. A distant yell followed by a scream gave Dubgetious the will to blink away the blinding lights and stumble to his feet. The footfalls came from a handful of hill warriors who ran at him up the trail. Their ragged breathing was harsh, their eyes narrowed. He noticed a body laying just paces from him. His throw had been true. A Masulian lay on his back with Dubgetious' spear standing proud from his chest.

Further down the trail, the surviving Masulian was surrounded by a handful of hill warriors. As Dubgetious watched, the rider was stabbed in the leg while simultaneously a spear rammed into his lower back. The rider's mount turned and kicked out with its rear hooves, knocking a hill warrior senseless to the ground.

Dubgetious lunged for his spear and pulled at the shaft. The Masulian's eyes opened and he tried to scream. Instead, a wave of bright blood erupted from his gaping mouth. Dubgetious cursed and stamped on the man's chest and heaved the spear which came free with a hideous sucking. He leaped back and levelled the spear as the hill warriors charged at him. One loosed a stone from his sling and the missile cracked into the spear shaft, the force stinging Dubgetious' hands and then the stone ricocheted into his chest. Gasping, he almost dropped the spear.

He tightened his grip and slashed his spear at the nearest hill warrior, a tall, rangy man wearing braccae tied at the waist and a mangy wolf skin over his shoulders. The hill warrior sprang back and gave him a yellow toothed snarl.

"I am Dubgetious of the Bastetani!" Dubgetious growled, his fighting spirit driving away the pain from his ribs. "I am going to gut you like the cur you are."

The hill warriors remained silent apart from their heavy breathing. Fanning out they circled him. Like wolves around a wounded stag. Their spears were crude things, but there were five of them. Dubgetious fumed at them as they trod in a circle around him, forcing him into the centre of the track so he could not break for the trees.

When they struck, it came faster than Dubgetious could imagine. In a heartbeat they closed on him, whipping at his knees with the shafts of their spears. He lunged and twisted, trying to bury his spear into their pox-scarred flesh.

A blow behind his right knee numbed his leg and he went down on it. As he did, he hunched over and swung his spear like a scythe. His reward was the sudden impact of his spearhead and a pained grunt from a hill warrior. The edge of his spearhead opened the flesh of the man's leg to the bone.

Then there was nothing more Dubgetious could do. A hill warrior stamped on his spear shaft, driving it to the ground while two more beat him across the back. Dubgetious let go of the spear and tried to catch one of those that swung at him. He missed, but the shaft slammed into his upper arm and he reared back in pain. If it had been a war spear, his arm would have snapped. A spear end was rammed into his gut and he doubled over, retching.

Rough hands clamped around his ankles as knees drove into his back, winding him further and forcing his face into the dirt. A strap of raw leather wrapped his wrists tight and he was dragged through the dirt while kicks were directed at his guts and sack. A stinking sandal of rotted leather and bark grazed his cheek.

"Not his face!" A hill warrior snarled while delivering a blow to the man who had kicked him.

"He is a fine one. Should last a few days."

Dubgetious was dumped on the ground where the scent of crushed leaves filled his nostrils. Branches stirred high above him as his hands were tied to a tree trunk. He gritted his teeth to quell the bowl loosening fear of the death that would be his. His eyes snapped wide when his tunic was ripped away and a bony hand pulled at his small cloth. The sight of the violated bodies of the couple outside the town walls came to him and he screamed in rage and terror. The hill warriors had raped both man and woman as they lay begging and screaming side by side. This was surely not his fate. His eyes clenched tight as tears spilled and he cursed them with his vomit sour breath.

Writhing naked in the dirt, he kicked out wildly, but this only drew laughter from the hill warriors who stood back to leer at him.

"Tell you what; he is a big bastard." One of them lashed him with a thin green twig he had broken off the tree.

"Go on! Hit him some more. Does good things to me when I hear them scream."

"Eat shit you worm. My shade will forever torment you and yours." Dubgetious hissed as he was whipped again and again.

The beating stopped and Dubgetious scrabbled toward the tree, pulling his knees close to his chest. Eyes wild, he stared at the ring of figures who were looking back down the track.

"What are they yelling? They killed their man now they want some of ours?" The yellow toothed hill warrior drew a foul gesture.

"Where are they running off too now?"

Dubgetious could see the hill warriors who had killed the Masulian disappearing into the wild growth alongside the track. They looked to be fleeing. He looked up the track towards the crest of the hill he would never reach. A figure on a horse was silhouetted there. His captors turned that way and stiffened with sudden gasps. Only the yellow-toothed hill warrior seemed unconcerned.

"One man on a horse and you are all shitting yourselves." He spat. "It will be one of those soft-arsed messengers from the big army to the north. Nothing he can do unless he wants to join his fellow here." He turned to Dubgetious with his teeth bared, one hand working the dirt fouled knot that tied his braccae around his waist.

The spear that grew from his chest wiped his smile away and turned his leer bloody. Before he could topple backwards, a dozen or more warriors in pale tunics and shining helmets burst from the trees behind Dubgetious and hacked the hill warriors down before they could utter a squeal. Dubgetious watched with disbelief as his captors fell dead at his feet. A blade appeared before his eyes, its point pressed into his cheek.

"This one to?" The dark-skinned warrior's lips peeled back in disgust as he looked Dubgetious over.

"Hold!" A burly man with a voluminous black beard appeared beside the warrior, his sword gripped loosely, dripping blood onto Dubgetious' feet.

"You speak Greek, savage?"

Dubgetious, the spear point pressing deep into his cheek and his neck over-extended, spoke with difficulty.

"I am a messenger." Fearful his response was not understood, he spoke more urgently. "For Hamilcar Barca. I am carrying a message to Eshmun."

The bearded warrior had taken pity on the Bastetani youth, escorting him to the village and presenting him to the Carthaginian leader, Eshmun. Dubgetious had delivered the message, retrieved from among his torn clothing, and been dismissed. Amma, the bearded warrior, was a Libyan and in charge of five hundred Libyan spearmen. He guided Dubgetious from the Carthaginian's pavilion with a hand on his elbow.

"Now. What to do with you?" Amma looked Dubgetious over. "You are a big lad and you know how to use a spear. Seems a waste to have you running around delivering messages."

Dubgetious gazed at the army of a thousand or more men, unsure of himself and uncertain what was expected of him now that he knew Berut wanted him killed.

Amma laughed easily. "Do not worry about this Berut. Some foolhardy Turdetani have overrun one of our mines and we are off to whip them bloody. If you wish, I will have equipment and armour assigned to you and you can fight with my Spears." Amma looked steadily at Dubgetious who slowly nodded and grinned.

Weak sunlight shed gray shadows over the scarred hills where mines had been bored into the earth and rock. Like guts torn from a carcass, the spoil from the mines was tipped haphazardly on the hillside below the mines, gleaming a sickly white after the rain that had fallen in the night. Trees felled in the hills were stacked in piles beside the mine entrances, to be used to shore up tunnels. The valley below the mines was a hive of dwellings, a few built of timber and many more of hide, some so rotted it was more tatters than cover. The reek of shit and rot hung over the place, rising in ghostly wisps from the many midden mounds and even from the shallow stream in which floated the bloated corpses of the mine overseers. A large force of Turdetani warriors still resisting Hamilcar Barca's rule had attacked the rich silver mine some days earlier.

"They threw the bodies into the stream from which they draw their water. What manner of fools are they?" Amma shook his head, his features twisted with scorn.

Dubgetious kept his lips sealed. His eyes were beginning to water from the stink and he did not wish for any of the tortured shades of the dead below to enter his body.

Eshmun had sent ahead his Masulian riders and a hundred Libyan warriors to block the trail to the north, trapping the rebels on the hill honeycombed with mine tunnels.

Dubgetious watched as the Turdetani warriors roamed between the lumber and mining spoil in tight groups, eyeing Eshmun's army of Libyans and levied Turdetani. The levied Turdetani showed no misgivings as they formed untidy ranks to the left of the hill. They were no sooner in place then they began to shake their spears at the trapped Turdetani warriors. These in turn called to them to join them in throwing off their Punic overlords. The jeering and shield thumping continued as the Libyans formed neat ranks three deep and some hundred warriors wide.

Eshmun sat his mount amongst a knot of senior warriors and hardly seemed to take notice of the warriors about to do battle. Instead, he chewed on dates, spitting the pips between his mount's ears, laughing at jests told. A drum pounded and the Libyans growled while the Turdetani levies whooped and shook their spears.

Dubgetious caught his breath when a half dozen Turdetani rebels threw down their weapons and ran towards their countrymen, arms outstretched and clearly calling for their lives. Only now did Eshmun take notice, his face turning to cold stone as he cocked his neck, like a vulture eyeing a meal. Dubgetious pitied the rebels.

"They are not to be harmed!" Eshmun flicked a hand at Dubgetious who turned his horse and dug his heels into its flanks. A messenger again, he reached the bottom of the hill and gagging on the stench, raced his mount to the front line of levied Turdetani, making for their Libyan leader.

"At Eshmun's command, allow these to live!" Dubgetious called loudly, pointing his spear at the cringing Turdetani rebels.

"Very well, Messenger." The veteran warrior shouted to the Iberian warriors he commanded to spare the Turdetani deserters even as Dubgetious was wheeling his mount away.

The remaining rebel warriors watched as the deserters were shepherded to the rear ranks. Many jeered their former companions, but it was lacklustre. The Libyan warriors began to move up the hill and the jeering ceased as the two hundred Turdetani and three hundred workers who had joined them shuffled into tighter groups, seeking courage against the overwhelming odds against them.

The Libyan ordered his levied Turdetani warriors to advance and a great bellow issued from their ranks as they charged up the hillside. Dubgetious regained his place beside Amma on the fringe of riders surrounding Eshmun and turned to watch the mismatched battle unfold.

The battle, if it could be called that, was short lived. The levied Turdetani struck from the left, shields clattering against their countrymen's and spears thrusting at living flesh. The Libyans split neatly into two blocks. From their rear came the first trumpeting calls of the war beasts the Carthaginians had brought with them from their distant lands. Emerging into sight from between hills came the swaying oliphants.

Dubgetious' jaw dropped at the sight of them. Their flanks and chests had been hung with heavy leather embedded with polished bronze lozenges. The tusks that curved forward from either side of their trunks were capped with iron and each beast carried two warriors wielding throwing spears.

The beasts were goaded into a swift run that shook the ground as they charged through the gap left between the Libyan warriors. Dubgetious glanced at the Turdetani rebels and the mine workers. They were backing up, mouths twisted with terror. Too late, they tried to scatter before the charging beasts, but they had backed into a tight press from which there was no escape except for the fortunate few at the very rear.

The oliphants plunged into the enemy, beating men and women to the ground with tusks and trunks. Swinging their great heads in wide arcs, they scythed deep into the press of enemy warriors, leaving behind a trail of crushed bodies and tangled limbs.

Close behind the war beasts, the Libyan warriors followed through, dispatching maimed warriors and cutting down small knots that had miraculously avoided being trampled and crushed.

The oliphants crashed through the enemy ranks, obliterating any resistance. Their role completed, they turned and trundled to the rear while the warriors perched on their backs loosed the last of their spears and arrows into the remaining enemy.

The tight bundle of enemy warriors and ill-equipped workers reeled and fractured into smaller and smaller groups as they were whittled down and driven back. Workers threw down the mining tools they had armed themselves with and dropped to their knees, beseeching their attackers for their lives, but to no avail.

The short fight turned into callous butchery, warriors taunting their pitiful victims before stabbing them through. Only three small groups still stood firm. These were centred on well-armed Turdetani leading men and it was clear they would sell their lives dearly. Two of these groups were assailed by the Libyan warriors while the third fought against the Turdetani levies. This latter group was giving ground slowly, backing towards a confluence of three mine entrances that opened onto a wide terrace carved into the side of the hill by miners. It was a good position for a final stand and once they reached it the Turdetani levies' numbers were useless as they could attack from only one direction.

The other two groups were shrinking with every heartbeat as their fatigued muscles strained to beat back spears thrust at them from every side. A final defiant scream signalled the mortal blow to the last Turdetani warrior in one group and then a bellow and crash of arms as the Libyans splintered and engulfed the second group.

Dubgetious, an eye on the third and last group who had claimed the terrace and were beating back their tribesmen, saw Eshmun nod with bored satisfaction at the success of the Libyans.

"Perhaps the leaders of this rebellion are among those that still fight. It would be good to take them alive to serve as an example." Eshmun spoke through his coiffured beard, his voice high. "The Turdetani levies lack the stomach to kill their own kind. Tell the Libyans to finish these last stubborn few and to capture any graybeards and leading men. Then they are to withdraw from the mines and any man found with unsmelted silver on him will be whipped and he and his tent mates will forfeit half their provisions and coin owed."

Again, Dubgetious made swiftly for the Libyan commander who was trying to rally his men, beating them with the flat of his sword until he had goaded them enough to charge.

The enemy Turdetani were pushed back to the very mouths of the mines they had liberated from Hamilcar. Others scaled the raw rock using handholds cut into it by the miners, escaping the vengeful spears of their kin and seeking refuge among mounds of loose spoil and logged timber. Still, the Turdetani rebels held and now they forced back the levied warriors.

The Libyans grinned bloody slaughter when they received the orders to round the hillside and kill yet more of the enemy. Hardened warriors, many with long seasons of battle experience, their losses had been slight while the Turdetani and mine workers they had faced had been slain to the last.

Dubgetious trailed Eshmun and his followers who rode close behind the rear ranks of Libyans. The dejected Turdetani levies filed away, their Libyan leader swaying with fatigue and bleeding freely from numerous wounds.

The Turdetani rebels numbered a hundred standing warriors and twice as many mine workers. They jeered the retreating levies and then the oncoming Libyan warriors. Spears floated into the sky and plunged towards the Libyans who roared and closed the distance between them at a charge. They crashed into the Turdetani, blades flaying flesh and smashing bone. A bitter stink of bile and shit rolled over the hill as bellies emptied and guts were torn open.

If the oliphants were a battering ram, the Libyans were a fire that spread and engulfed the enemy. The clash of iron, splintering of wood, and rip of leather and skin rose to a crescendo and then fell away sharply. The Libyans occupied the terrace overlooked by the three mine entrances. They dragged upright any enemy warrior that could stand, bound them and sent them flailing off the edge of the terrace to be tied together. That done, they departed with wide, empty grins, supporting their injured and carrying their handful of dead.

Perfumed linen held to his nose, Eshmun led his entourage onto the corpse bedecked terrace. Dubgetious looked with curiosity at the timber framed mine entrances that led into the heart of the hill, following the trail of silver bearing ore. He rode closer and squinted into the dusty darkness, but it was impenetrable. He circled the terrace, keeping close to the raw rock walls where he could. In places, he was forced to skirt mounds of rock that had broken off the cliff side and tumbled to the terrace. This seemed to happen frequently for there were many such mounds. Dubgetious saw rocks and dirt spilling in a widening stream from the hillside above the cliff and decided staying beside the walls was a poor idea. Better to risk the blade of a warrior feigning death than be crushed by a landslide of rock.

A deep rumble built quickly into ground shaking thunder. Rocks bounced and rolled down the hillside above the terrace, crashing to the ground and splintering with vicious cracks. Alarmed and then terrified, Dubgetious' mount reared and bucked him clear from her back. He fell heavily, his landing cushioned only a little by the bloodied corpse of a Turdetani warrior, her glazed eyes vacant in death. He heard other mounts neighing, their riders equally unable to remain seated, falling. A boulder bounced once and then flattened a rearing horse, crushing both it and its rider. Rising, Dubgetious grabbed his spear and began to run for the safety beyond the terrace. Behind him, a new danger followed. The stacked tree trunks had come free of whatever restraints had held them and were rolling and cartwheeling down the hill.

He flinched away from a near miss as a log drove into the hard rock at his feet, sending splinters flying. Eshmun was rolling away from an oncoming log, but another was close behind. Dubgetious swerved and caught the Carthaginian under the arm, dragging him to his feet with a grunt and wheeling him away from the spinning tree trunk. Shoving the Carthaginian ahead of him, he saw others less fortunate, driven into the ground by the avalanche of timber and rock. A dark shadow fell over him and Eshmun and Dubgetious slammed his shoulder into the Carthaginian's back, knocking him over the lip of the terrace as a huge boulder swept over them.

The rumbling dwindled and died, leaving the air swirling with dust and his senses reeling. Raising his head, he saw the savage destruction on the terrace and winced at the shuddering bodies of men who had been too slow to react.

Layered in dust, Eshmun coughed raggedly and scrambled to his knees, eyes unfocused. Other survivors were rising and seeing Eshmun, began to gather around him. Amma appeared and helped the Carthaginian leader to his feet, smiling at Dubgetious.

"Tanit's hand has saved you!" Cried a weeping rider, his helmet dented and bloody dust plastering his beard.

"The Bastetani Messenger did a fair job too." Amma pointed out. He had his back to the mines and was dusting down the Carthaginian.

Dubgetious bent to retrieve his spear once again and felt the rustle of wind part his hair as he did so. The thump of a spear into flesh was followed by a gurgled grunt of surprise. A score of Turdetani graybeards erupted from the mine shafts. Leaping across shattered boulders and splintered lumber, they roared their battle cries.

The surviving riders were virtually unarmed. Swords, when dragged from sheaths, were bent or shattered. Spears had been dropped in the flight from the avalanche which now seemed part of a trap laid by the rebels.

"Run!" Dubgetious screamed, dashing forward to leap onto the terrace. Amma was at his side in a heartbeat, a spear with foreshortened shaft gripped in his fist. Two others joined them, grabbing frantically at partially buried blades of dubious quality and wresting them from the death grips of their former wielders. A handful of battered riders minus their mounts were trying to hustle Eshmun to safety, calling for warriors to attend. The Libyans were already racing their way, having seen and heard the avalanche of rock and timber. It was clear they would not arrive before the Turdetani were upon them.

Chapter 11

The cold did little to dampen the stink of the Punic army camped across the southern slopes of three hills. Lyda wrinkled her nose as the north wind lifted the odour of a thousand improvised latrines and funnelled them towards the tree line where her and her companions sheltered. Her eyes narrowed as she watched a hundred horsemen range through the valley below and as it became apparent that they would pass, she looked back to where Chalcon crouched, watching her. He grinned confidently.

"It is as you predicted." She allowed. "The Barca army is readying to storm the Oretani town."

He shrugged. "The town has good walls, but without stout-hearted defenders to man them, it will fall."

"The Oretani will know that." Lyda reflected on the desolation of her own home settlement. The warriors and home keepers killed, and the fittest of the survivors levied by force into the Barca army. She had no great love for the Oretani, but she would not wish such a defeat upon them at the hands of Hamilcar Barca's army.

"They will fight harder if they believe Orissus is coming to their aid." Chalcon made a fist, knuckles white beneath dark hairs.

"I am not here to save the Oretani. I wish only to find my son and bring him home." She glared accusingly at Chalcon.

"If only it were that simple, eh?" Chalcon's grin faded and his eyes sharpened. "Barca has spread from Gadiz through the Turdetani lands, turning proud graybeards and leading men into levies." He shook his head. "If you were told three seasons past the mighty Turdetani would be so humbled would you have believed it?"

Lyda did not respond for it was unnecessary. No one would have believed it. The Turdetani were numerous and well-armed. Their warriors raided at will and on those occasions when their leading men combined, they laid waste to settlements of neighbouring tribes until ransoms were paid. Now. Now they were a beaten people.

Chalcon read her expression. "Save your son, but for what future fate?" He pointed at the huge army. "Until Hamilcar is beaten, there is little future for him. He will be killed or levied along with all the rest of the Bastetani's best warriors."

Lyda turned away from Chalcon, her lips pressed into a thin line. She wanted no part of this, but recognised she had little choice. Chalcon's words rang true. Hamilcar Barca of Carthage led his army across the land, destroying or taking all that was Iberian.

Chalcon rose silently and walked to her side. "I must get into the town, Lyda."

"It is madness." She glared at him. He flashed that white-toothed grin of his. He was a bold and handsome warrior with the blood of heroes in his veins undoubtedly. "What can you, one man, do for the Oretani trapped there behind their walls?"

"Hope is a powerful weapon, Lyda. I can give the defenders that."

"While I deliver what they hope for?"

"You better than anybody. Orissus will hear you. Convince him to raise his Spears and lead them against Hamilcar Barca."

"No more levies." She whispered.

When Cenos had found Tascux on the hillside he was laid out on his back, head thrown back and mouth hanging slack. He looked like the body of a warrior whose shade had fled. She stepped beneath the slight overhang of rock and looked down mournfully into his face. Her scream when he opened his eyes drew the others in moments.

They sat around a small fire, Lyda's Bastetani and Chalcon's Greeks, laughing with Tascux at the tale.

Never a great speaker, Tascux harrumphed and grumbled when asked to tell them how Cenos had wet herself, thinking he had returned from the dead.

"The enemy riders were below me and some other buggers were creeping around in the grass, so I found a dry spot and..." He shrugged.

Even Lyda was amused and prompted the taciturn old warrior. "A dry spot and... come on, Tascux."

Muttering through his tangled beard, he dipped his head. "I fell asleep."

The warriors slapped their thighs and howled. Chalcon shook his head, eyes watering. "That is the tale of a true graybeard! The enemy all around and unconcerned, he takes a nap."

Passing around a basket of roast goose shot from the sky that afternoon, the warriors' faces flickered in the orange glow of firelight. Lyda ate sparsely, her stomach too knotted to feel hunger. When daylight came, they would be in the midst of the Carthaginian camp. The thought left her dry-mouthed, but she was committed. They had watched as hundreds of Iberian warriors came and went from the extended lines of the enemy encircling the Oretani town. It was true that these were mostly Turdetani or Turduli, but there were others too. Greeks, Libyans, and Gauls. There were dark-skinned men and red-haired giants. There were women dressed in skins and men wrapped in robes. This was truly an army drawn from all nations that resided beside the Inland Sea. It was the factor that made Chalcon's plan feasible.

With a simple tilt of her head the talking and laughing ceased. Lyda lifted a waterskin and upended it over the small fire. Dipping her fingers in the wet ash and warm mud, she painted a wide band of black and gray across her face. The others followed and soon they all wore blackened faces. Now they passed a small cup of congealing blood mixed with vinegar from hand to hand, daubing bloody patterns through the ash and mud, smearing it over bared chests and between breasts.

"We have spoken. All here know the danger and we accept. May Runeovex guide us, but remember that tonight is not a time for battle, but for cunning."

She glanced around at the waiting warriors. Despite the cold, they had stripped off all armour and wore only simple tunics belted at the waist and their sandals wrapped to their knees. Likewise, they carried only spears. The few swords the group possessed were wrapped in cloaks and buried. Now they looked nothing like Bastetani or Greek warriors, but like any savage fighter welcomed into armies such as the one led by the Barca.

Chalcon stepped into the centre. "This is a thing we must do. We have seen the spread of these Carthaginians and their Punic ways. It does no good to think of this as a battle the Oretani deserve or not. What Hamilcar Barca does here in the days ahead will happen to every village and town across Iberia." He clapped his hands suddenly. "So let us warriors of Sucro and our Bastetani companions make this a lot more difficult for him."

He grinned, as he must have done when a boy and planning a raid on the cook's stores with his friends. Lyda nodded once and shouldered her spear. Her bare arms, stained by ash and her hair thick with mud, she looked like one of those rough and savage people that lived beyond the fringes of the tribes and were drawn to war like wasps to blood.

She would not let Chalcon lead, but allowed him to stay at her shoulder with the rest of their small company following. Ranging through the night, she led them to the darkest part of the Carthaginian camp, treading warily lest they stumble into a circle of sleeping warriors.

The camp was vast with no discernible pattern to where warriors had set their sleeping places and except where cook fires still burned or voices murmured, it was all but impossible in the dead of night to see the sleeping figures until almost upon them.

Lyda backed up a step, noticing at the last moment the sleeping figure at her feet. Chalcon hissed softly and pulled her by the elbow to the right. Irritably, she twisted her arm from his grip. His teeth gleamed in the dark as did the whites of his eyes. She suspected he was enjoying every moment of their tense journey through the Carthaginian army.

Rounding the sleeping form and a handful more, she made directly for the flickering torches kept alight along the town's walls. Before they could reach the walls though, they would have to pass through the ring of sentries that guarded against surprise attacks from the town's Oretani warriors.

She grunted at the sight of a large fire and the dozen warriors that stood close to the shedding warmth. More such fires burned at regular intervals around the entire town, leaving no way to reach the walls without passing through the light cast and within view of the alert sentries. To her left, on a slight incline, were lines of shadowy tents, crouched like beasts waiting to pounce. The remnants of an olive grove stretched to the right, the trees stripped and many felled to feed the army's cook fires.

"This is where we part." Chalcon murmured into her ear.

Lyda eyed the town walls a spear's throw beyond the sentries.

"You will not have long."

Chalcon knelt, the sound of leather being tautened told her he was tightening his sandal straps. When he stood, he placed a hand on her shoulder, his skin rough with callouses, hers grainy with mud and ash.

"Bring Orissus' Spears, Lyda."

She nodded and turned away wordlessly, leaving the warrior from Sucro to slip away into the dark.

Taking her companions and those of Chalcon, she made for the rows of tents, readying herself for what was to come next. At the outer wall of the last tent where the light from the sentry's fire traced the barest glow, she passed her spear to Audoti and signalled to Tascux. Reluctantly, the old warrior handed his spear to Cenos.

"What is wrong, old friend?" Lyda whispered, with cold humour. "Would you prefer I took Audoti or Eppa?" She snatched his hand and dragged it to her breast, forcing him against her flesh, pulling the tunic clear, so that the hard bud of her nipple pressed into the centre of his palm.

"Lyda... this is too much!" He protested, his voice gruff and loud in the dark. A muffled curse sounded from within the tent.

Lyda grinned and slapped Tascux a resounding blow across his cheek, snapping his head around.

"If you want what I have, you will need to try harder!" She raised her voice, using the Greek of her old hometown.

Warriors within the tent were waking with curses while one or two who had heard her words, laughed. A man shouted in broken Greek. "She wants it harder! If you cannot manage, bring her here!"

Lyda could tell Tascux was bristling with anger and she regretted having to do what she did next. She lifted her knee, catching him squarely in his manhood with just enough force to cause Tascux to grunt and stagger. He hooked a foot under a tent rope, shaking it violently.

"It is working, but you need to do more." Cenos hissed, her eyes on the sentries at the nearest fire. Some were peering their way, others still shuffling around the flames to keep warm. "Slap her, Tucsux. You will only ever get this one chance."

Lyda cursed. The tent's occupants were wide awake and she heard the curtain being thrown aside. They were coming to see the fun. She pulled her tunic loose from the belt and allowed her breasts to fall free, pale skin mottled with drying blood. She backed away from where Tascux was rising and signalled to the rest of the company to spread out. They did so quickly, melting into the dark like so many shades.

Backing away from Tascux, she edged towards the sentry's fire and cackled. As the first of the warriors from within the tent appeared, seeking the cause of the commotion, she called to the sentries.

"His spear has gone soft! I have seen slings harder than what he offers!" She slipped her hands under her breasts and lifted them, cackling again. Deliberately, she twisted and spun, closing on the sentries, allowing the firelight to catch her form and light her chest and thighs. She had their attention now. They were all watching, sidling around the fire to stare and voice opinions. More than one lifted his tunic and thrust with his hips, making vulgar suggestions.

Her companions were emerging from the dark, mingling with the tent's occupants and others awakened by the growing noise. Audoti, with Cenos at his side, stalked through the warriors. Those who did not see him were shoved from his path. Breaking from the milling group, he strode into the firelight, a scowl fixed on his wild face, his hair pale with ash and skin streaked with blood. Warriors cursing him for shouldering them, swallowed their words at the savage sight he made.

"Come!" He growled at Lyda.

She had not seen Chalcon move and could not be sure where in the shadows he crouched. She needed to be sure he had slipped past the sentries who were still clustered close to their fire.

She spat at Audoti and edged towards the devastated olive orchard. Her companions fanned out as though to capture her. Warriors hooted in anticipation of violence. She had moved closer to the sentries and Audoti bellowed again for her to come, advancing on her with his spear resting over his shoulder.

The leading sentry lifted his own spear and strode towards Lyda, calling his fellows to heel. Their eyes danced between Lyda and Audoti and the barbaric looking woman with him.

"Come keep us company by our fire, woman." The sentry called to Lyda, his smile wet and crooked.

Audoti swivelled his spear off his shoulder and levelled it at the sentry. "Not yours. Ours!"

A shadow flicked briefly through the outer edge of the firelight, unnoticed by all save Lyda who had been watching for it. She tucked herself back into her tunic, eliciting groans of disappointment from the men watching. She threw a gesture at the sentries and turned her back on them, striding towards Audoti. Chalcon was past the sentries. Her role here done.

The leading sentry snarled and lunged at her. A shadow form hurtled into him, sending the surprised man staggering into his companions. Tascux held a spear before him, its wicked edge hovering close to the sentry's eyes.

Lyda shouted and the sentry's companions charged. In a heartbeat, the night was filled with curses and blades.

Chapter 12

Dubgetious sprang. A splintered tree trunk lay before him, wedged between tumbled rocks and bloodied by the carcass of a mount crushed beneath it. He landed and immediately braced as a large Turdetani, wild with battle fever, leaped at him.

Dubgetious twisted and slipped to one knee, slashing his spear across the warrior's forward leg. The blade opened the leather and wool of the man's sandal, not reaching flesh, but tripping him off balance. The warrior carried a round shield and he battered Dubgetious in the face with this as he fell across the tree trunk.

Ears ringing, the Bastetani youth struck out with his spear, again slashing at the warrior with the edge of the spear's long blade. This time, he opened the man's exposed thigh, cutting to the bone. The warrior screamed and rolled awkwardly, blood painting the tree. Amma silenced him with a vicious stab to the throat, spraying more blood into the air.

The rest of the Turdetani were on them and Dubgetious dodged behind the tree trunk to avoid a massive blow from a falcata, a dreaded weapon able to cleave helmets and spill brains. The falcata bit deep into the tree, sending splinters of wood spinning. Dubgetious rose and stabbed with his spear, aiming at the man's groin, hoping the falcata had stuck fast in the wood. It had not and the warrior snapped his wrist back, deflecting the spear thrust with ease. Dubgetious lurched aside to avoid the return swipe which swept past his face with the scent of grease and wood sap.

Amma cursed as he slipped on the blood slick tree which had become the barrier between the combatants. A spear thumped into the wood beside his cheek and a moment later lifted as the Turdetani wielder readied to plunge it into the Libyan's ear. Dubgetious, too far to lunge, hurled his own spear, sending it cracking through the warrior's ribs and exploding blood in a fountain from the warrior's gaping mouth.

Amma rolled to his feet and ducked another swipe from the warrior with the falcata. The unmounted riders that had joined them to slow the Turdetani and allow Eshmun to escape, were hacking and slashing, surrounded by the Turdetani who had erupted from the mines. They screamed in panic and frustration as blade after blade flicked at them, cutting through their minimal armour, opening limbs and then torsos. Sobbing, a rider fell against the tree trunk, a spear buried in his gut, and was immediately seized by howling Turdetani. Screaming in terror, the man was hauled bodily over the tree and set upon. Dubgetious with little battle experience felt his legs weaken at the brutal sounds they made as they killed him, horrified by the man's terrified pleas and screams. Sickened when the screams became grunts and gurgles, knowing that even then, the rider still lived.

The warrior wielding the falcata, grinned at Dubgetious and Amma. His face a storm of pox scars and broken veins. Eyes glowing with cunning blood thirst, the Turdetani feinted to the left and then the right. Grinning at the pair as they flinched. Dubgetious was tugging frantically at a spear shaft half buried beneath the tree and the horse crushed beneath it. The mount kicked suddenly, its senses returning. The movement allowed Dubgetious to withdraw the spear.

"Come on you ugly camel's arse!" Amma shouted at the Turdetani, brandishing his spear valiantly. With the shaft snapped, it was no longer than the Turdetani's falcata and no match at all.

Dubgetious snapped a hurried glance back to see how far the Libyan warriors were and if Eshmun had reached safety. Too far and not yet. The last rider howled as a blade found his ankle, severing the cord there with a snap that twisted his leg horribly.

Dubgetious lifted his newly won spear and grimaced. The blade was folded along one leaf and shivered loosely on the thick shaft. One blow and it would snap free.

The Turdetani stopped feinting and with a roar, leaped the log, hacking at Amma who thrust his spear out. The falcata was the chosen weapon of Iberian champions; forged to bend when needed, it rarely snapped and the hungry curve of its blade struck with the force of a battle axe. Amma cursed and fell back, his broken spear spinning away to fall far beyond reach.

Dubgetious saw the rest of the Turdetani turn their way, hungry for new kills. He crouched, his feeble spear held underarm in his right hand, his left hand splayed on the loose dirt. The Turdetani warrior narrowed his eyes, calculatingly. Amma was little threat while Dubgetious was still armed. He spat at Amma and leaped at Dubgetious. The Bastetani youth roared and sprang, flinging out his left hand as he did so. It was an old trick and ugly. Gravel and grit flew at the Turdetani's wide-eyed face and although little struck the warrior, just enough dust to water his eyes found their mark. Dubgetious saw the other Turdetani quicken to their companion's aid and wasted no time in attacking. He had one chance with the precarious blade. With all the might in his powerful shoulders and the keen sight of his youth, he plunged the blade into the warrior's neck, beseeching the God of Spears, Runeovex, to allow him to open the warrior's throat. The blade sank into the side of the man's throat and then twisted. Too late, Dubgetious tried to flick it and open the great artery buried there, but only succeeded in twisting the shaft free of the blade, leaving it buried a quarter of its length in the man's neck.

Amma shouted in fear behind him and his heart thundered like a valley of drums. Thinking only of a swift death, Dubgetious spun the heavy shaft and cracked it across the Turdetani's helmet. The man snarled and snatched at the shaft, narrowly missing it. He drew back his sword arm, readying a gut-skewering thrust. Dubgetious' eyes were fixed on the spearhead protruding from the man's neck, bobbing as the warrior roared blood and hate at him. He swung the shaft, eyes narrowed.

Thunder and dust. The world swept around Dubgetious, tilting from blue to gray. Blows hammered him across hard rock until he fetched up against a warm form wedged beneath the tree over which so many blows had been struck. His hair, bloody and matted, covered his face so he could see only blurred figures and swinging sandals. The form beneath him moved and he was thrust painfully aside. The log above him trembled, dust falling across his body. His senses sharpened, filled with the stink of horse and blood. The mount crushed beneath the tree was still alive and now scrabbling frantically, its screams of pain loud in his ear which he jerked away from its snapping jaws.

Its kicking had startled the Turdetani warriors and one man lay clutching a snapped leg. Dubgetious saw them moving away from him and then he felt thunder rising through the ground. Expecting at any moment to be crushed by more falling rocks and timber, he was too startled to identify the next thumping sounds until a Turdetani warrior crashed to the ground paces from him, his jaw opening and closing as thick blood flowed through his beard. The throwing spear that had felled him was still quivering from the force of the impact.

Sliding away from the unfortunate horse's death throes, he wiped his eyes clear and peered up at ululating Masulians.

Amma lay beside him under a canopy erected beneath a tree upwind from the mines. The warrior was smiling, teeth loose in his mouth and lips split, but smiling. At the foot of their cots, Eshmun was dragging a painted fingernail through his freshly combed beard, teasing the tight curls. The Carthaginian's eyes were moist with unshed tears.

"Tanit herself stood over us, permitting no killing blow to land." Amma nodded. He looked at Dubgetious and winked.

"You should have seen the Bastetani here swing a blow."

Eshmun cleared his throat. "We have all seen the warrior he killed. Truly his hand was guided by the gods." Eshmun turned his gaze on Dubgetious who winced as he tried to lever himself upright.

"No, lay back. Your bones should be in splinters, but they are not." A shade of a smile breezed across the cold Carthaginian's features and his expression softened. "You were willing to sell your life for my safety. This is no simple gesture and so no simple matter to reward." He dipped his head in a gesture of gratitude or respect. "Is there some boon you desire?"

Dubgetious, uncomfortable, glanced at Amma who nodded. Dubgetious' eyebrows rose in uncertainty.

Eshmun grunted with vanishing patience. "Well?"

Amma spoke. "The Bastetani, Dubgetious that is, wishes to bear a sword." Amma's grin slipped a little and he added hurriedly, "I would be happy to train him to use it without cutting off his... er, his toes."

Eshmun frowned. "We have swords. Is this all Dubgetious of the Bastetani wishes?"

"A falcata. The one the Turdetani tried killing me with." Dubgetious found his voice. "It seems fitting."

Amma gaped at him and Eshmun's depleted retinue whispered, but the Carthaginian nodded, surprising them all.

"It is fitting. It is yours if you give your oath to fight for Carthage."

Dubgetious blinked, his joy tempered by this unsought bond.

"To fight for Carthage? Very well."

Chapter 13

Unarmed, Lyda dove away from the grasping arms of a squat sentry, his mouth wide and leering. Her companions were stabbing aggressively at the sentries, keeping them at bay. No blood had been spilled as yet, and the swelling crowd of warriors from the nearby tents regarded the events as a diversion, urging them on with hoots and insults. Lyda kicked the squat sentry's legs from under him and rolled to her feet in time to plant her foot in his face.

Tascux was crouched low, his spearpoint held poised to thrust into the face of the leading sentry. He growled a warning when the man slid his hand towards his fallen spear, stilling the motion at once.

Lyda grinned and drew her short knife, holding it similarly to the throat of the squat sentry.

Speaking in Greek, she addressed them all. "Save your blades for the enemy who even now could be stealing towards us." She jerked her head at the walls of the town and was rewarded when the sentries glanced over their shoulders, suddenly aware of the darkness that lay beyond the firelight and between them and the enemy walls.

She pressed her blade against the squat sentry's cheek, watching the whites of his eyes grow. "Another time perhaps?" She grinned at him, the firelight painting her blood-smeared face with unearthly savagery. "Back away." She called to her small group who backed up three paces before lowering their spears and turning for the deeper dark. Tuscux had not moved, so she slapped his shoulder.

"Come. We have done enough."

The leader of the sentries watched her with suspicious eyes, but remained still as Tuscux stepped back. They turned and raced into the dark after the others, leaving the watching warriors to moan and curse the sudden end to their entertainment. The leading sentry called after them, anger stretching his words.

"I will find you! The army is not large enough to hide you from my men and I!"

Lyda felt Tuscux eyes on her in the dark. "What?"

"Might make finding our kin a little difficult?"

"If we meet him and his lot again, it will go badly for them." Lyda reached the others who were making their way back along the route they had followed through the army.

Cenos noticed her at once. "That was too close!"

"It worked did it not? I saw Chalcon pass the fires unseen. He will be over the walls by now. Besides, no one got hurt." She glanced at Tucsux. "Well, almost no one."

There were sniggers from the companions and Tucsux growled and gave them an evil eye.

They bedded down within spitting distance of a large clan of Gauls and awoke at dawn to their strange language booming across the lines.

"Bastards are loud. What are they on about?" Audoti complained.

"Who can tell? They are from far to the north." Tucsux shrugged his shoulders and rolled to his feet to better see their neighbours.

Lyda sat up, hair still caked with mud and ash, her face equally smeared. She rubbed her cheeks and frowned.

"We should wash at once so none recognise us from last night."

"I will fetch water." Tucsux took up their waterskins and used the water remaining in them to douse his head. He rubbed vigorously at the mud, ash and blood. Eppa, grimaced at the mess and grabbed a waterskin from his hand. "I will pour while you rub."

"The gods! It is cold." Tucsux complained as water dribbled from his long hair down his spine.

Eppa smiled. "The mighty Tucsux complaining. I never thought I would hear that."

"This is not the season for war. Real warriors should be at their hearth fires, counting their victories, not freezing their sacks off."

"Hamilcar of Carthage is a new enemy and brings with him a new meaning to war." Lyda intoned. "There will be others fetching water, Tucsux." She did not need to tell him to keep his chin down.

The warrior grunted and shook his head, scattering water and splashing Eppa who squealed.

"Bastard!"

He grinned at her over his shoulder, making for the stream.

Hair cleaned and tied back, Lyda signalled for Tucsux to follow her. The Herb Queen gathered her satchel and joined them.

"It is not necessary for you to come." Lyda eyed the young healer,

"Oh, a Herb Queen can always be useful." She smiled and stepped ahead.

Lyda looked at Tucsux who spread his empty palms, equally nonplussed.

The Gauls numbered in the hundreds. They were large people, with loud voices and exaggerated gestures. Tucsux, who was among the biggest of the Bastetani, would be considered of average size among them. Those women among them were all much larger than Lyda. The few swords they were honing were far longer than the blades used among the Bastetani. Likewise, their spears were longer and thicker, the blades like short swords. They were clustered in groups, every man and woman talking at once it seemed. Every warrior there was dressed for battle; heavy with leather, padding and chain.

"Looks like they are readying themselves for a fight." Tucsux observed.

Lyda nodded, her eyes straying to the larger Carthaginian camp. Similar activity was occurring throughout Hamilcar's army. She cursed. The Oretani town may be overrun before midday, long before she could summon Orissus and his spears.

The Gauls noticed them and began to exchange comments among themselves. Lyda drew back her shoulders, alert for any hostility and felt Tucsux beside her do the same. The Herb Queen dogged their footsteps in silence.

A burly warrior shouldered his way from the centre of a large group, his armour of the highest quality, scrubbed and polished to a gleam in the early morning light. His white moustache hung like plaited horsetails from his cheeks to his chest, bright beads of bronze and silver threaded into the trailing ends. He bore a spear in the crook of his arm, and a sheathed sword hung from under his shoulder, the tip reaching to below his knee. A graybeard and champion.

Speaking the Greek patois used throughout the trading ports of the Inland Sea and the lingua franca in the Carthaginian army, the Gaelic graybeard addressed them.

"What do you seek here, Iberians?" His question was directed at Tucsux, who cocked his head at the Gaul, but remained tight lipped.

"Greetings, I am Lyda of the Bastetani. We are newly come to fight for Hamilcar and…" she opened her arms at her sides, palms up. "Number just a handful. We seek to fight at the side of your warriors."

The Gaul shifted his gaze, his eyes traveling up and down Lyda's body. He shook his head slowly and then more deliberately.

"Bastetani, eh? Eager to spill Oretani blood! Well, this is the right place to be. Today we will crush that town of theirs." He swung his spear to point at the Oretani town walls. "You cannot fight beside us. Your Commissar should have allocated you a position. Speak with him." The warrior grunted and began to turn away.

Lyda looked blankly at him for a heartbeat before catching his meaning. Her face darkened with anger. "We are not levied!" Her words snapped like a whip. "We come of our own free will as proud Bastetani warriors."

The Gaul paused midway in his turn and looked back at her, his great brows creased. He allowed his spear to slide through his hand until it was balanced for a thrust.

"The Bastetani are at war with us, yet here you are with no Commissar?" His eyes narrowed and he levelled his spear at Lyda's chest. "How many of you dog turds are there?" Gaelic warriors stood closer, their conversation dying as they scented the tension in their graybeard.

Lyda saw the mistake her pride had led to and her mind raced to find a way to allay the warrior's suspicions. "It is true many Bastetani clans are at war with Hamilcar. My companions and I wish to join his great army not die fighting it. We are just twelve, but all seasoned in battle."

Her words had no effect on the graybeard, instead, he grinned through clenched jaws.

"Look at me, bitch! Do I look like a suckling? I can smell a liar across a hall filled with farts. And right now the stink of liar is heavy in the air." His spear punched to within a hair's breadth of Lyda's throat. "I think it is time you wore chains and knelt before our Commissar."

Tucsux growled, but already he was surrounded, spears bristling at him. Lyda sent an invocation to Runeovex. If ever she had need of the spear god's power, it was now.

In answer to her hurried prayer, the Herb Queen stepped forward, loosening her hood and letting it fall to her shoulders. She lifted her chin so her face was lit for all to see. At once the Gauls made hurried gestures to ward off witchcraft.

"Your Commissar pays you in silver, yes?"

The Gaelic champion eyed the elaborate swirls etched into her brow, the shock of white growing among her raven black hair and he swallowed at the sight of the necklace of bones taken from the hands of each foetus and newborn she had sacrificed. Uneasily, the warrior grunted a confirmation.

"And the Commissar is rewarded in silver for the warriors that swear to fight for the army. He pays a part to those warriors and keeps the rest, growing wealthy."

"Of what concern is silver to a… healer?" He had groped for the word, preferring it to the obvious.

"Oh, none. More an interest to you I would think for what if you became our Commissar? Would you not then be paid in silver for our pledges?" The Herb Queen smiled serenely at the big warrior, unconcerned by sharp blades dripping dew at her feet.

The warrior squinted at her, shaking his head. "Cunning and pretty. You know how these Carthaginians deal with spies?" He grimaced. "They set you on a pyre of wet wood, feet in an iron cauldron." He spat. "Nasty way to die. Days it takes. Cooked to death. Your flesh swells and parts from your very bones. By the time your shade flees, your legs from the knees down are white bone."

"I suppose these Carthaginians also dine on your boiled flesh while you scream on your pyre?" Her voice light with mirth.

The graybeard scowled. "Laugh now, but a pretty little thing like you will have uses before they set you to boil." He grinned at her and Lyda. "You too, although you look a little sour for my tastes."

"As a Commissar you could earn good silver for adding our spears to yours. You know this, but there is something else, is there not? That you long for?"

The warrior rocked from one leg to the other in agitation, his face growing long. He eyed the Herb Queen for an uncomfortably long heartbeat before swallowing and easing his grip on his spear.

"You are young, but are you gifted?"

The Herb Queen smiled in answer.

Lyda, brought her companions and those of Chalcon to the lines of the Gauls where they marked their places and strung mean shelters of thin hide on lines of braided hemp. The promised battle had been delayed by downpours that fell from the black clouds that rolled together above them, battling one another with thunderbolts and lightning shafts.

"She is returning!" Eppa had been anxious for the Herb Queen's safety, fretting from the moment Lyda and Tucsux had described their encounter.

They all sprang to their feet, rushing to surround the healer as she approached.

"What ails the graybeard? What did he require? Tell us."

"You know I cannot speak of such things. No one would come to me with their ailments and needs if they knew I would tell their enemies." Her smile and the bright spark in her eye roused their interest even more, but they relented as she sat before the fire in the least smoky part of their rough shelter.

With a sigh and a longing look at the gruel Eppa was stirring into a beaker for her, the herb queen shook her head. "I cannot speak of the warrior's needs, but it will take some days for me to make a potion and stir powerful shades from their slumber to do my wishes."

"He is our enemy, so surely you can tell us what his need is?" Cenos hissed.

In a voice as stern as winter hail, the Herb Queen replied, "Do not seek that which I will not offer, Cenos."

Chastened, Cenos dipped her chin, her lips suddenly bloodless with fear. The others were silent, faces contrite at their behaviour. The Herb Queen was right to withhold the man's woes from others, even them.

She smiled and thanked Eppa for the food. Testing it, she found it too warm and blew the thick porridge.

"While with the Gaul, I heard something of Hamilcar's plans. Perhaps if I told you this, it would appease your hunger for gossip?"

Lyda's head snapped up, her expression eager.

Chapter 14

He stumbled and tripped. Falling to his knee, his shield rim battered into his cheekbone, sending a bolt of pain through his face. Yells and calls of derision forced him upright, swaying in the cold autumn wind.

"Come on, Bastetani! What use is all that muscle and blade if you cannot land a blow?" Amma's voice called from behind him.

Dubgetious whirled about, his newly gifted blade scything the air before him. The forged iron edge was wrapped tightly in raw wool and hide to prevent injury, but the weight of the blade could still crack bone. The weight! He had held the falcata for the first time just that morning and was stunned at the heft and balance. Now though, after a morning of wielding the heavy chopping blade, his wrist ached and his arm and shoulder muscles were knotted.

"If I put a sack over your head, you might fight better." Amma taunted. The Libyan, as battered and bruised as Dubgetious after their battle with the Turdetani, seemed to soak up the punishment. He had promised to teach Dubgetious how to master the sword and so far had simply taught Dubgetious how little he knew. The few postures and moves his father had shown him were nothing in comparison to what the Libyan could flaunt.

Determined to walk away with at least one good blow landed, Dubgetious took a deep breath and blinked his frustrations away.

"I am ready." He concentrated, keeping his feet spaced beneath his shoulders, his blade held low and angled away from his body.

Amma grinned and lunged. Dubgetious braced his shield and swung his sword, but the Libyan had done something with his feet and was not where Dubgetious expected him to be. He was within a hand's breadth of him and the covered tip of his own sword was at Dubgetious throat, resting on the rim of his shield.

"Hear that?" Amma asked, his breath smelling of dates, warm in Dubgetious' face.

"Hear what?"

"The sound of Bastetani blood splattering the ground." Amma laughed aloud and danced away. "Enough!"

Dubgetious clapped his sword against the face of his shield.

"I know less now than I did when I started!"

"I disagree!"

"Amma! What manner of lesson is this?"

The Libyan smiled at Dubgetious and then his face became solemn. "It is the most important lesson of all, young Bastetani. You have learned that you know naught of fighting with a sword and that in battle you would die ten times over."

"This is important? I asked you to teach me how *not* to die. Better yet, how to kill."

Amma rested his sword over his shoulder and turned away. "I am hungry. Come eat with Kelle and I." He looked back at Dubgetious. "She has a wonderful way with bruises as well."

His wink was unnecessary. Dubgetious found his feet already following. He had seen Amma's long-limbed woman and found her almost as beguiling as the Herb Queen.

Eshmun's column joined with Hamilcar's army outside the besieged Oretani town two days later. Two days in which Amma had sparred with Dubgetious each morning and evening; teaching the Bastetani youth how to brace, hold, thrust and pivot. Dubgetious, determined and eager, had learned much, but knew he was still a poor sword wielder. The muscles of his arm had grown stiff and he knew he had to keep training to gain the strength and skill needed to wield the impressive blade. He quenched thoughts of the oath to fight for Carthage stubbornly, not ready to contemplate that.

Hamilcar's army hunched low on the hills surrounding an Oretani town, wet and squalid after four days of heavy rains. Cook fires raised a blanket of smoke over the camp that stubbornly resisted the breeze.

That evening Amma led Dubgetious to the pavilion of the Master of the Messengers, Berut. Dubgetious felt icy sweat on his brow at the thought of meeting Berut and proving he was still alive. They arrived and the curtain was swept aside. Too late now to change his mind for Berut had already seen him.

"Ah, Bastetani, you survived the journey!" Berut dismissed a trio of young messengers with a curt command and then rose, his eyes flicking to Amma who squeezed into the tent behind Dubgetious. The tent was larger than Amma's and comfortably furnished with a small attractive table of ivory and dark red wood around which were arranged plush cushions on thick carpets. The wind whistled through gaps in the hide and a drop of icy water fell on Dubgetious' cheek.

"I did, no thanks to the Masulian guides you provided to ensure I reached Eshmun."

Berut tapped his cheek with a long finger. "You escaped them obviously. Impressive." The warrior from Sulci noticed the sheathed sword at Dubgetious' side and his eyes darkened. "You have permission to wear a sword?" He looked at Amma.

"Eshmun's gift to Dubgetious. I am named Amma."

"Greetings." Berut quickly recovered his surprise at hearing that Eshmun had bestowed a gift on Dubgetious and gestured at them to sit. "This is an interesting development. You are full of surprises young Bastetani. One moment offending notable Carthaginians and the next inspiring them to lavish you with gifts."

Dubgetious polished the grip of his sword with his palm for a heartbeat. He had been cautioned by Amma against telling of how close Eshmun had come to being slain as this would reflect poorly on the Carthaginian.

"Eshmun is truly fair and rewarded me the sword for killing an enemy champion. I am honoured by it and have given my oath to use it against his enemies."

"A great honour. Eshmun is not known for being overly generous." Berut glanced at Amma.

"Eshmun requests that your Messenger be released and reassigned to serve with my Spears." Amma lifted a well-greased fold of worked leather from within his tunic. "As a token of his appreciation for allowing this." He held it out.

Berut grunted, leaned forward and took the leather wrapping with two hands, dipping his chin. He placed it before him on the table and tight lipped, began to unfold it cautiously, fearing a deadly trap. He flicked aside the last corner of leather to reveal a heavy broach. Lifting his eyes to Dubgetious and Amma, he nodded in appreciation while tracing the intricate patterns in the highly polished silver and gold.

"It is a fine piece. I see no harm in having you feed off Eshmun's provisions rather than mine, but you will still report to me."

Amma inclined his head. "I will convey your appreciation to Eshmun, however I believe he intends Dubgetious to serve as a warrior within his inner circle. It is, I am sure you will agree, a more fitting role for a promising warrior."

Dubgetious held his breath. Amma had advised him that Berut had a final say on the appointment that Amma had weaselled from Eshmun. The broach was not even from Eshmun, but came from the collected wealth retrieved from the slain enemy Turdetani, part of which was divided among the warriors.

Berut fingered the broach silently for a long moment, his eyes skipping from Dubgetious to Amma. At last he shook his head and sighed. "By Tanit, who am I to stand in the way of one so highly regarded as a warrior?" He folded the broach away in the leather and slipped it into a satchel at his feet. "Visit often, young Bastetani. I pay well for good information."

Dubgetious released his breath and glanced at Amma who grinned at him.

Amma leaned forward. "How long does Hamilcar plan to campaign in this blasted weather? That is information I would like to know." He made a show of pointing to a splash of rain that had landed on the low table around which they lounged.

Berut grinned. "You and every other sorry bastard in the great Punic army." He wiped away the offending droplet with the palm of his hand. "I usually sell information, but since it is you asking and it is common knowledge…", he shrugged and continued, "Hamilcar insists on ransacking the unfortunate little town he has encircled and possibly even marching on the Oretani stronghold to the north."

"So why has he not done so yet? It looks like the army has been here for days already and the town's defences cannot be so formidable." Dubgetious spoke.

"The gods. Thunder and lightning. Rain." Berut grunted, waving his hand at the roof. "What warrior wants to risk being burned to his sandals by a lightning shaft aimed from above. The gods are jealous of their wars."

Amma nodded. "And archers cannot loose their shafts in the rain. It would be hard work taking the walls without archers covering the men climbing ladders."

"It will be even harder if Hasdrubal carries out his threat to withdraw his forces to Gadiz." Berut held up a hand. "You never heard that from me."

Dubgetious pulled his cloak tighter about his throat to ward off the brisk wind as they trudged through the foetid mud running between the tents. He eyed the torches that guttered on the walls of the Oretani town, wondering what those behind the stones were thinking. The Oretani were not likely to throw open their gates without a bloody fight. The smoke that had hung over the army had been dispersed by the wind which had also cleared the clouds. Bright stars glittered in a sweeping arc through the deep black of the night sky.

"You have your wish now, Dubgetious. You are no longer under Berut's thumb." Amma turned towards his tent.

"I owe you my thanks, Amma. I loathed being a Messenger." Dubgetious made to follow the Libyan.

Amma halted him. "Your freedom comes with a price."

Dubgetious' jaw clenched. "The broach?"

Amma laughed. "Not that. Your obligations. You are to stand watch until relieved. At the central pavilion." He laughed at Dubgetious' expression. "It gets better. You will be assigned a tent and will be required to sleep there with a half dozen other hairy-arsed warriors."

Dubgetious grunted, unamused. "You will still train me? To wield the sword?"

"Of course. You are a slow learner, but I never give up." He laughed at Dubgetious' outraged expression and held up his hands. "No, you have learned much already. Once your arm and feet begin to retain the moves, you will become much more skilled." The Libyan clapped Dubgetious on the shoulder. "Best get up to your post."

While he was walking towards the central pavilions that housed the upper echelons of the army, the sun appeared, casting a vivid rainbow against the storm dark clouds to the east and lighting the camp for the first time in days. It reminded him of the Herb Queen and her claims that she drew shades through the arc of colours.

The following day the sun rose into a cloudless sky, burning through the mist in the lower folds of the hills in a short time and raising the army's mood.

Dubgetious watched through eyes swollen from a lack of sleep as warriors emerged from their waterlogged tents and threw cloaks and tunics over bushes or strung them from tent ropes to dry in the sun. He slipped in the mud and lurched against a wagon of provisions being unloaded into the eager hands of a rough looking band of red haired warriors.

A spear butt jabbed him forcefully in the ribs. "Hands off our provisions you thieving shite!"

Short tempered with fatigue, Dubgetious clenched a hand around the shaft and pulled hard as he turned to the voice, his free hand already at his sword's hilt.

"I am Bastetani! No thieving shite!" He turned fully, coming face to face with a wall of chest muscle. It was little wonder the spear's owner had not stumbled or given when he pulled the spear. The Gaul was a full head taller than Dubgetious and his chest was as wide as that of a bull's.

"Bastetani, eh?" The warrior looked down at Dubgetious, the Greek patois ill-formed behind his long facial hair. "There are more of you lot around than lice on a man's sack." He shoved Dubgetious backwards. "Get lost before you lose your teeth, suckling."

Cursing inwardly, Dubgetious glared at the huge warrior and his fellows tossing amphorae, sacks and baskets of oil, cereal and cured meat from the wagon. He began to back away and then hearing a familiar sounding voice, paused. In a heartbeat, the huge Gaul stepped forward, his spear held like a stave across his muscled belly.

"Get lost means disappear from my sight."

Dubgetious forgot the voice, ducked a lazy swipe of the spear shaft and retreated. He resisted the urge to throw a jibe back at the big warrior. He had left childhood behind when he had fought and lost at his village.

Chapter 15

There was discord in Hamilcar's great army. Hundreds of levied Turdetani were stealing away by night to return to their valleys and kin. Provisions had been in short supply for three days and men and women were hungry, cold and falling ill. Lyda watched as blades were drawn and blood spilled over the slightest insult. Her companions roamed where they could among the wider army, reporting back all they heard and saw.

"Grain enough for half a meal of bread and nothing else." Cenos, ever quick to find fault, grumbled as she tipped the weevil-infested grain from a sack onto a wooden board.

"They say there are a hundred wagons loaded with provisions just a day's walk from here." Tascux spoke as he drew his spear blade along a whetstone and tested the edge against his thumb.

"They have been saying that for three days, so someone is lying." She began to sift the grain, flicking stone, wood chips, and rat shit from it. The weevils and grub worms, she left.

"The rain washed away the trail and they are bogged down to the axels in mud. The drovers and herdsmen are sitting on their arses in a sea of slime, drinking and eating all our provisions." The bitter comment came from one of Chalcon's companions and heads all around bobbed in agreement.

Lyda crouched nearby, only half listening to her companions' words. It had been three days since Chalcon had gone over the wall to the Oretani and she knew she should have left already to seek out Orissus, the greatest of the Oretani leading men. She would have, except that on the second day, while combing every part of the huge encampment, her heart had lifted when she heard a Bastetani warrior cursing and rounding a wagon stuck in mud, had come face to face with a man from her village. The man had raised her hopes, telling her Dubgetious had been separated from the others of the village and taken away to be trained for some duty. Torn between her promise to Chalcon and finding her son, she had remained another day. She would leave to find Orissus soon, but in the meantime, Tascux's words had given her a fresh idea.

Dragging Tascux aside after their meagre meal, she whispered, "These wagons with the provisions, do you think there is truth there?" They were alone among the warren of pens used to hold livestock to feed the army; all empty now.

"I do. It makes sense that Hamilcar would have provisions sent up from the south by wagon. After all the rain, they will be slogging through a sea of mud."

"Then the gods have gifted us this opportunity. We should find the wagons and burn them." Her voice was hard with retribution.

Tascux considered the idea in silence before shaking his head.

"They will be well guarded and if there are even half the number of wagons they say, then the drovers and herdsmen alone would outnumber our small company."

Lyda smiled grimly. "We only need to burn some few of their total. The losses will make Hamilcar reconsider his position and he may decide to retreat."

Tascux nodded slowly. "That we can do. Strike like lightening out of the dark."

"We will need to move tonight. The rain has ceased for now and the wagons may already be on the move."

Night came swiftly and throughout the encampment, hungry and despondent warriors curled up under their cloaks to escape their misery. Lyda and her companions watched as the Gauls banked their fires and wrapping themselves in furs, settled down to sleep. They followed suit, prepared to sleep for a short while and then steal away. The sentries guarding the camp were more alert after a number had been punished for sleeping and allowing many levied Iberian warriors to desert. Lyda was confident they would be able to slip past these though.

The great army was silent under a thin gauze of mist and smoke. The only light was that cast by the sentry fires and torches burning in the inner circle where Hamilcar and his leading men plotted their war.

The Bastetani woke and rose silently as one. Their movements stealthy as they stepped through the dark, a dozen formless shadows. There was no movement from the Gauls who snored as loudly as they spoke.

Leading her companions towards their mounts, Lyda saw a form step from behind the horse lines followed by another. Her heart beat loudly as sharpened iron caught the moonlight. Her companions hissed as all about them, Gauls materialised from the dark, spears levelled.

"You thought to slip away in the night, Bastetani. Do you know the penalty for that?" The Gaul, their commissar and the Herb Queen's patient, strode towards her. A torch flared brightly followed by several more. They were surrounded and outnumbered.

Hearing the sudden clamour of her companions and sensing their own blades lifting, Lyda held her hand up.

"Hold!" She cast a meaningful look at her people before turning to the Gaelic warrior. "We are hungry. You know this. We go to find provisions."

The Gaul grinned. "You go to burn our provisions is what you mean."

Lyda's mouth opened in surprise. Had they been betrayed? Surely none of her people had done this, but perhaps one of Chalcon's?

"Your face condemns you, Bastetani. You will be taken alive to the Carthaginians. The rest we will kill here." He raised a fist and his warriors hummed from the back of their throats, preparing to kill.

"We planned to burn just a few wagons to cover our tracks. Make it look like hill riders from the Turdetani." Lyda shouted desperately.

"Liar! Kill them!" The Gaul swung his spear, slamming the haft into her head.

Staggered by the blow, she fumbled for her blade, but her vision was clouded and her ears filled with a roar.

Spears lifted and shields cracked around her as the Gauls attacked her small group. Another blow slammed across her shoulders and she toppled to the ground, hearing Tascux's anguished roar as her senses failed.

Dubgetious, lifted his chin, breaking from his faraway thoughts. The clang of blades carried on the night wind. He was on sentry duty in the middle of the night once again, the wet wood smoking moodily in a brazier, doing little to warm him.

"Do not piss yourself, Bastetani." A deep voice called from nearby. "It is no doubt just a few deserters caught trying to sneak away."

He shivered despite the heavy coat he wore over his padded armour. He had seen tens of deserters executed that very morning and their deaths were humiliating and excruciating. Conditions among the warriors must be extreme if men and women were prepared to risk such deaths.

"The sun will be up soon. You ready for what is to come?" His fellow sentry stepped closer, his armour gleaming and his flat face a darker shadow in the night.

For a moment, Dubgetious thought he meant the execution of the deserters until he remembered. Hamilcar planned to storm the Oretani town the following day.

"I am." He rubbed the crafted hilt of his sword although he knew he was unlikely to be included in the warriors sent to attack.

"Not the fighting bit. They will not send you, yet." The Libyan sentry laughed. "The fun afterwards? When we get to ransack the place?"

Dubgetious saw Beratza's face as she fell. Heard her screams fade to gags and retching before gurgling away to silence. He blinked and let his blade slide back into the leather covered wooden sheath.

The sound of fighting had given way to a few yells and hoots and for their sakes he hoped the would-be deserters had died quickly.

Hamilcar Barca sat his mount at the front of a thousand warriors. The eastern sky was birthing the sun of a new day and the Carthaginian warrior had his face lifted, eyes closed and nostrils flared. Breathing in the power of dawn.

Dubgetious sat his mount silently, his mood dark as the night just past. Drums began a slow beat and the silent ranks of warriors, Libyans, Turdetani, Greek and Gaul, began to clap their spear shafts against their shields.

Rousing himself, he looked across the ruined fields towards the walls of the Oretani town, lined with warriors, their spears held ready. He imagined the cold fear coursing through the men and women standing there and preparing to sell their lives dearly to keep their kin free.

Amma's mount snorted and pranced. "Now, now. You like a good fight, eh?" He patted her neck affectionately and cast a glance at Dubgetious.

"What is it that has so soured on your tongue then?"

"Is it true that Hamilcar ordered no lives spared?" Dubgetious asked.

Amma grunted. "True, but even so they will not all be killed. Those who survive the fighting and looting will be taken as slaves. He wishes the next Oretani town to know that resistance means death."

The drum beat had quickened and lifted, the massed warriors were roaring and then moving. They spread across the terrain, shields held tight to their sides, spears swinging like pendulums. There would be other towns and villages once this one had been raised. Hamilcar would not rest until every Oretani was pinned beneath his heel.

A flurry of movement on the town's walls saw a thin cloud of arrows lift into the air. They caught the sun's rays at the apex of their flight, glinting as they hung for a brief moment there before swooping towards the onrushing army.

The arrows did little against so many. Warriors snapped them from their shields or saw them glance from their armoured chests. Some few caught one in the flesh of the face or neck. The killing only truly begun at the foot of the walls.

By midday, Hamilcar's army had had enough. A ridge of dead were piled at the base of the town wall. Shattered ladders protruded from between tumbled corpses. Blackened skulls leered out of crushed helmets. Smoking pyres of corpses lay where they had fallen, burned by fired oil.

The Carthaginian leading men stood in a circle, fists on hips and faces red. Hamilcar Barca was unmoving, head lifted towards the town walls. Words were raised and then Hasdrubal spun away from the General, calling for his mount.

"He will not send any more of his warriors to the wall." Amma's voice was grim. They had sat together through the morning watching the warriors' vain efforts to either scale the walls or smash through the gates. "He will go back to Gadiz now and leave Hamilcar with half the number of warriors."

Ignoring the observation, Dubgetious turned to Amma. "Why not use the oliphants to breach the gates? They are armoured and strong enough are they not?"

Amma laughed. "Always thinking, you!" He shook his head. "They are far too clever to be used so. They would shy away from the gates and present their flanks to the enemy." His face clouded. "It would be a terrible waste."

Dubgetious laughed bitterly. "The oliphant, it seems, are wiser than the three hundred dead warriors laying at the walls. And more valued."

He jerked at his mount's reins, wanting to be away from the place. Amma's hand closed on his arm.

"Look!" The warrior was staring at the gates of the Oretani town which were swinging open. From within, a single man exited.

A hush fell over the Punic army as he appeared, every eye following the solitary warrior's steps as he strode purposefully out of the gates.

Looking at Hamilcar, Dubgetious saw the warrior leader nodding, a smile of victory creeping across his lips. The Carthaginian turned to the leading men clustered at his back and he caught sight of Dubgetious. He pointed at the Bastetani and cocked his finger. Dubgetious dismounted hurriedly and made his way swiftly to Hamilcar.

"You are the Bastetani who was rewarded by Eshmun are you not?"

"I am. Dubgetious of the Bastetani." Dubgetious was bewildered that Hamilcar knew this.

Hamilcar nodded. "I remember you. Dubgetious, son of Venza." He scratched a louse from his beard and cracked it between his thumb and finger, eyes still on Dubgetious. "Yes. You will do very well. Accompany me."

There were protests from the Carthaginians and one, a youth younger than Dubgetious even, spat at him while another of similar age made to slap him. A third stopped them, stepping between Dubgetious and the others.

"Respect your father's command if you wish respect in return." Hannibal, son of Hamilcar, waved Dubgetious on with a grim smile.

Lengthening his stride to make up the distance, Dubgetious followed Hamilcar Barca across the bloodied battlefield to stand before the Oretani's single envoy. Hamilcar was already talking when Dubgetious stopped at his shoulder, ignoring the feeble gasps of a dying Turdetani nearby, he stared at the envoy. Dressed as an Oretani, a bloodied gash over his cheek to prove he had fought on their wall, the man stood tall and proud.

"We seek to hear your terms. If they are within our means, perhaps we can end this bloodshed."

Hamilcar grinned. "My terms are what I originally offered, except I will now have five hundred more warriors from your town."

The envoy's eyes flicked to Dubgetious and recognition flared in them.

Chapter 16

Cool water trickled through her lips, tasting of wild spring grass and sun. She reached her hands towards the burning orb in the firmament, feeling its promise of life strong within her. As she did, a dark cloud appeared and covered it. A thousand and more ravens swirling above her, their talons raking her arms and their raucous cries thundering in her head. She gave a great cry and flung herself at them, determined to feel the warmth of the sun again.

"Hush! Now, hush. They will hear you and come." The frantic whisper reached her.

"Herb Queen." Her voice was hoarse. Her heart hammered and she came close to emptying her stomach.

"Drink." The young woman pushed a clay bowl into her hands.

Lyda lifted it to her lips, thirsty beyond imagining. She drank until it was dry, her eyes darting around the latticed branches that formed the cage in which she was imprisoned. She let the cup fall and clenched her fists. All her companions dead and her son forever beyond her reach now.

"You must wonder how the Gauls knew your plan?" The Herb Queen's question brought Lyda's face up. So, someone *had* betrayed them.

"A couple of children, those feral creatures that sleep among the livestock, heard your talk of burning wagons and taking provisions. They sold your words for a bowl of soup each."

Lyda sighed with relief. She could not have stood to learn that one of her companions had done so.

"As for the Gaul, I will tell you what ails him. An evil shade entered a wound in his thigh and settled in his sack. He makes taking a piss sound like birthing a child." The Herb Queen's eyes shone in the dark.

"He punishes you as well?" Lyda had not included the Herb Queen in her plans to raid the Punic supplies and was saddened that the young woman might be punished.

"No. He dare not. I have been able to weaken the grip of the Shade and the bastard can stand now when he takes a piss." She gathered her cloak tight about her as wind keened through the cage. "Dubgetious is alive, Lyda."

The words were like a breeze on a dying ember, lighting Lyda's spirit. She gasped.

The Herb Queen smiled, her beauty appearing as though from behind a mask. She caught Lyda's hand and raised it to her cheek where a tear flowed. "It seems he has found favour with the Carthaginians."

"My son. He serves them willingly?" Her voice hitched. "Tell me you know of a way I can escape here and find him." Lyda's face took on a new determination and she gripped the Herb Queen's hand fiercely.

"Warriors will come to release you at the night's darkest. They are from our village."

"What of Tacsux and the others?"

The Herb Queen shushed her. "They are slain. Lyda, you made a promise to Chalcon. Honour that promise and go to Orissus. Tell him that half the Barca's army has retreated. Now is the time for the Rising of the Spears."

"And Dubgetious? What of him?"

The Herb Queen fixed Lyda with a hard stare. "The gods willing, you can find him afterwards, but before then, Hamilcar must be defeated."

The Bastetani warriors came as promised. Silent as lynx, they swept through the dark, opening the throats of the few slumbering sentries and cutting the cords that held the cage door fast.

There were just eight and all carried the same haunted look as they dragged Lyda free and cut the bonds that tied her hands and feet.

Only one spoke. "Lyda. Greetings."

"Thank you. Are you remaining here, or will you accompany me?"

"We have had our fill of this place. You wish to go to Orissus?"

Hardening her heart, Lyda nodded. "That is what I must do."

"Then we should go now."

They stole from the camp in short, creeping bursts, wary of the sentries patrolling the margins and foregoing the lure of the horse lines. They would have to go on foot and with very little by way of food.

Once beyond the lines of Hamilcar's depleted army, they quickened their pace, using the feeble glow of the moon to track a path through steep rock and thorn growth. Creatures scuttled from their path and once they heard a boar and piglets crash away from their presence.

"Wonder there is a living thing left. Seems we have eaten every kind of creature these past days." The speaker grunted.

"We are heading east not north towards Orissus' stronghold." Lyda was watching the stars and moon.

The warrior in front of her waved a hand forward. "There are more of us waiting.

She had taken a spear from a slain sentry along with his belt and short knife. Now she gripped the spear tight, wary of a trap, but her caution was unnecessary. A night jar called and the warrior adjusted his course, making for it.

Lyda frowned in recognition, but followed mutely. Moments later two figures rose from behind a thorn bush, faces pale in the moonlight.

"Lyda?"

Tucsux embraced her tightly and as he did, she felt his body stiffen with pain.

"You are injured!" She pulled away in concern.

"My arm. It is surprising how difficult killing Gauls can be." Tucsux replied. Lyda shook her head and turned to the second figure.

"Cenos? You live."

"Does not feel like it. I am injured to, so do not expect a hug." The warrior nevertheless stepped forward and hugged Lyda.

"Just the three of us then?" Lyda whispered.

"That will have to do. Besides, we have these eight who are hungry for revenge." Tucsux grinned in the dark.

"You are right. It will do. No horses though, can you manage?"

Cenos snorted. "We eat Gaelic iron and shit it out like iron filings. Can we go now?"

Lyda laughed, her mind cleared and her heart beat with a warrior's pride.

"To Orissus. Let us bring his Spears down on this Thunderbolt from Carthage."

The gates of Castulo behind them, the small party of weary warriors savoured the smell of cooking, of oils and meat. The aroma of baking loaves flooded their mouths with saliva as they strode forward, surrounded by the burly, well-armed Oretani warriors that had found them a day's march south of the Oretani city.

The Oretani leading man stood when they rounded the corner and came to an open court outside his large stone and timber home. Orissus was a shorter man than Lyda had imagined he would be, but what he lacked in height he made up for with a chest few could close their arms around. The cold wind did not seem to trouble him for he wore only braccae. Unusual, but no doubt learned from the Celti people to the north.

One of the Oretani warriors escorting Lyda and the others went ahead of them and spoke quietly to Orissus who listened while watching her approach.

She stopped two paces from him and ground the butt of her war spear into the chipped rock ground.

"Greetings, Orissus. I am Lyda of the Bastetani."

"Greetings, Lyda of the Bastetani." Orissus voice was rich with confidence. A good voice for turning minds and hearts to his will. "You come from the south I hear. How fares our foe?"

"Poorly. Will you fight him?" Lyda had thought long on what to say to the leading Oretani warrior, the man that could raise tens of thousands of Spears with one word. The words she spoke were not what she had planned.

The Oretani warriors escorting her stood as still as mountains. The hands and tongues of the women and children sewing garments nearby stilled. The hairless cur lounging beneath a broken handcart stopped licking its sack.

Orissus leaned forward from his ankles. His eyes bored into hers and then he straightened and flexed his great chest.

"Can I defeat him, Lyda?" His voice remained even, no insult taken at her abrupt challenge.

"His army has halved. He has maybe three thousand Spears."

"He has oliphants. He has two thousand horsemen as well." Orissus answered her, proving that he had eyes on the Punic army and knew their numbers as well as she.

"All hungry. All facing a wall they have not breeched. Put your Spears on the hills above them and they might fight, but it is more likely they will retreat." She spoke candidly, suspecting the Oretani would respect nothing less.

"My warriors do not fight in the winter. It is not right to summon them from their valleys and hills to die in the cold season."

Lyda lifted her spear, causing consternation among the watching warriors, but Orissus stood unmoving. She pointed at the watery sun behind a veneer of winter cloud.

"There are no seasons while Hamilcar Barca tramples us beneath his heel, turning our very kin against us."

"You speak of the Turdetani fighting now for the invader. They are poorer of spirit than I credited them."

"My people too have been made to fight his war. My son even."

Orissus grunted. "You are hungry I think. We will feed you and your few warriors."

"We would rather starve than eat with the man who allowed Hamilcar Barca to rule us."

Curses erupted from Orissus' warriors and more than a few stepped forward, anger etched on their broad faces.

For the first time, Orissus smiled. "Lyda of the Bastetani. How could I face my dreams if I allowed you to starve?" He stretched his arms wide. "You want me to send Hamilcar Barca's shade screaming into the lands of the dead? Very well. I will raise a great host of Oretani Spears." He brought his thick-fingered hands together with a thunderous clap and smiled again, the skin around his eyes folding. "First though, we eat."

Chapter 17

Black mud sprayed from around the warrior's body as he slammed backwards into a pond of stinking water, sword spinning away and eyes rolling backwards. Dubgetious did not hear the blast of breath from his lungs nor the choked cry as the man landed. He was already wheeling to his left, bent low over his left knee, shield and falcata slashing to that side as one weapon. Warriors cheered as another fighter crashed to the ground, his legs cut from under him, his face a mask of pain.

Standing upright and letting his shield and sword hang at his sides, Dubgetious smiled at the three men as they sat rubbing their bruises.

"That is half your provisions for the week that you each owe me." He nodded to the men in turn. "Well fought."

Looking at Amma who stood, arms folded and wearing a broad grin, Dubgetious stripped the leather padding from the blade of his falcata and slipped it into his scabbard.

"You have learned fast." Amma clapped his shoulder. "That is six wins in two days."

Dubgetious patted the hilt of his blade. "I have a graybeard from the Vascone to thank. His advice is sound."

Amma's eyebrows rose. "What advice did he offer that I could not?"

Dubgetious drew his blade and held it at eyelevel, tracing a finger from the thin waist along the ever-widening body and up to the tip.

"The power of the blade is here." He retraced his finger to the wider edge halfway along the length. "To harness its power, I must swing the blade freely and in a fight, the best way to do so without being struck in turn, is to use the shield alongside the blade."

"I saw how you did that. I thought it foolish at first, but the shield caught your opponent's blade leaving room for your own to land." He smiled in appreciation.

"There is more to master; the placing of my feet and shoulders. Watching the opponent's eyes and knuckles."

"Knuckles?"

"Every warrior will tighten their grip the moment before they swing." Dubgetious grinned and swung his falcata in a dizzying display, his confidence writ large in his expression.

"Now you are simply showing off." Amma reproved him, but his tone was light.

A string of twenty Masulian riders galloped past, hollering and ululating, mud hurled high from their mounts' hooves.

"Where are they off to?" Dubgetious asked.

"To reinforce the warriors escorting the wagons bringing our next meal. There was a rumour that some of our levies had planned to burn them to prevent the provisions arriving." Amma stared after them.

"Hamilcar intends to remain? Even after Hasdrubal's departure?"

"He scents victory. The Oretani are well fortified, but there are too many of them in the town."

Dubgetious frowned and shook his head. "Both are reasons to expect defeat rather than victory."

"Think, Dubgetious. You have a sound mind." Amma gave the Bastetani youth a hard look.

His stomach growled and he heard the now distant drumming of the Masulian horsemen on their way to bring in the much needed supplies to feed Hamilcar's army.

"I think I see. The town's provisions are enough to feed its own citizens through winter and until the next harvest. The many additional warriors trapped there will quickly eat through their stores."

"Hamilcar expects the town's leading men to arrive at this conclusion before many more days pass. They will then have a choice of starving or submitting."

"They are a hardy people. They may choose to starve."

"Then before that happens they will become weak and our warriors will cross the walls." Amma took Dubgetious by the elbow and drew him closer. "You are on sentry duty again tonight, yes?" he went on quickly. "There are more rumours. Plots to kill Hamilcar." He made a distasteful expression. "Hunger and cold has a way of leading good warriors astray. Keep your eyes open and challenge anything that looks suspicious."

Dubgetious frowned, alarmed at the intensity of Amma's tone.

"I will."

Amma nodded grimly. "See that you do for if such a plot succeeds, it will go badly for those on sentry duty."

Nightfall brought a bitterly cold wind that whistled through the bedraggled tents and hastily constructed shelters raised by the warriors of Hamilcar's army. Men and women hunkered beside fires built with green wood, trying to coax some warmth from the hissing piles. Their rations were barely enough to keep them alive in the cold let alone to fight on.

Dubgetious was fortunate enough to enjoy a bowl of broth with a hint of meat in it, doled out to the sentries arriving at the great Carthaginian general's pavilion to stand watch through the night. With both hands cupping the bowl, he sipped slowly while eyeing the comings and goings of servants and messengers.

From within Hamilcar's pavilion came the sounds of laughter intermingled with the chords of a lyre. For some there was no shortage of food, drink and warmth. Dubgetious nodded to his fellow sentries as they arrived and hurried a servant to fill their bowls.

Light spilled from the pavilion as a curtain was thrust aside, followed by a figure draped in a heavy cloak. With Amma's warning still fresh in his ears, Dubgetious watched the figure approach the huddle of sentries. He slurped the last of the broth, belched and threw the bowl to a servant boy.

The approaching figure signalled to him. Dubgetious put his hand on his sword hilt, straining to see who it was as he stepped from the huddled warmth of his fellows.

"Your cloak, sentry. I would trade you for mine." The man undid the glittering broach holding the cloak closed at his throat and shrugged it off.

Dubgetious grew more alert. "My cloak is worn almost through. Why would you want it unless to disguise yourself?"

"You are right, I wish to disguise myself, but for good reason. I commend your observance."

The voice was familiar, but the speaker took care to keep his face from showing in the light of the fire. Wary, Dubgetious took a step back, his hand tightening on his sword.

"Who are you?"

"The son of the man you guard so fastidiously. Will you swap your cloak for mine or shall I ask another?" The man stepped to the side and showed his face briefly.

Dubgetious recognised the youth at once. He was truly the son of Hamilcar. Releasing his sword hilt, he fumbled to release the feeble pin at his throat and throw off his cloak, threadbare and rank.

"Why would you wish to disguise yourself and in a cloak as poor as this?"

Hamilcar's son grinned and thrust his thick cloak into Dubgetious' hands.

"I know your face. You are the Bastetani warrior favoured by Eshmun."

Instead of recoiling from the stink of Dubgetious' cloak as the Bastetani expected, the Carthaginian smiled and took a deep breath.

"There. How do I appear?"

"Like a poor levied Bastetani warrior." Dubgetious answered. "Your sandals are a giveaway. No levied warrior owns such. Best swap them for my own as well."

Hamilcar's son released a rich laugh. "Oh, I think not." Dubgetious could barely believe he had tried to entice the son of the great Carthaginian general to part with his sandals.

"I had to try. You would do the same."

Hannibal laughed again. "Indeed." The Carthaginian turned into the dark, making for the greater camp and the ordinary warriors that suffered there.

"Who was that?" A Libyan sentry asked through a mouthful of broth, eyeing Dubgetious' cloak with narrowed eyes.

"A warrior that owed me a cloak." He smiled and patted his new garment, inhaling the heady scent of wealth that rose from it. He turned and looked out into the dark, concerned suddenly for the safety of the foolish Carthaginian. He turned back to the scowling Libyan. "How about we trade cloaks? Yours for this one and to even the exchange you cover my post. I will not be gone long."

Heartbeats later, wearing the Libyan's lice infested cloak, Dubgetious set off to follow Hannibal Barca. It took no time to catch up with the Carthaginian. The sun had sunk beyond the world of mortals and the cold night had sent most warriors and servants scurrying for shelter. Hannibal was one of the few still about, stealing from shadow to shadow on his secret quest. Dubgetious followed discreetly, shaking his head at the Carthaginian's furtive movements. They signalled deceit and cried out to be challenged. He was not though and Dubgetious was puzzled when several times Hannibal drew close to cook fires to warm his hands, exchanging brief greetings with the warriors huddled around.

After several more such stops, Dubgetious joined the group of warriors around the same fire Hannibal had chosen. He nodded to the men beside him and keeping his chin tucked low, eyed Hannibal from the corner of his eye.

Presently a warrior coughed and spat a glob of phlegm into the smoky fire where it sizzled and danced.

"That is what I think of this winter war. Evil shades lurk in the mist and ride on the north wind."

Others nodded and a woman sketched a rude gesture at the pavilions illuminated by the sentry fires.

"Hamilcar and his lot are warm as shit up there. Plenty to eat as well. While we sit here starving and frozen."

Dubgetious risked a glance at Hannibal, keen to see his reaction to the dissent among the warriors. Hamilcar's son stood casually, his hands stretched to the flames, blackened with mud. The youth must have dirtied them to better blend in. He made no remark, but nodded along with the others.

Hannibal lifted the hem of his cloak to his throat and turned from the fire. Dubgetious waited a heartbeat and followed. They were headed closer to the Oretani walls and the Punic sentry fires that surrounded the town. Flickering torches guttered at intervals along the walls and he wondered how the Oretani sentries and warriors fared. He envied them the shelter of stone and timber buildings on a night as foul as this.

He slowed and peered ahead. Hannibal had disappeared. Cursing, he lengthened his stride. He passed a wagon turned on its side, wheels and axels long cannibalised and the rest stripped to the framework for wood. A ragged hide was tied to the remains forming a shelter of sorts. The stink of unwashed bodies was strong and he saw several pairs of eyes watching him from under the hide. These were camp followers. People of no name who did any task for coin or salt or less.

"Did you see a warrior pass this way?" He called.

There was a rustle and a hand appeared from the dark, filthy palm open. Dubgetious fished the meanest copper from the purse within his tunic. "A copper for the direction."

The hand formed a fist, a single finger pointing. Dubgetious glanced that way and saw nothing. The hand was clicking thumb and finger impatiently. Dubgetious grunted and dropped the copper.

Walking quickly in the direction indicated, he saw only more servants and camp followers. Just as he was beginning to think he had lost Hannibal, he heard the distinctive thump of a curtain falling into place to his left down a line of tents. He turned that way on a whim and passed the tents slowly, eyes squinting to see any tell of Hannibal's passing, be it a fresh sandal imprint or shivering tent curtain.

It was the light and the smell that alerted him. The light burned pale against the dark silhouette of the tent, shining from the small rents in the hide where stitches had been made to join the walls. It was the light of a lamp and few warriors would bother to spend coin on the oil to burn. The smell was a lingering scent Dubgetious recognised from the cloak Hannibal had given him.

He searched the dark shadows beyond the tent and seeing no watchers, moved closer. Voices murmured within the walls of the tent and Dubgetious strained for long heartbeats to make out the words. It was fruitless and in time the wind died, but the cold was leeching through his sandals and up his legs. He shifted and blew into freezing hands, undecided. He would need to return to his duties soon. About to leave, he noticed the timbre of the voices change and almost before he could react, the curtain was lifted aside and someone hissed. "Kill the lamp first, fool!"

The light was snuffed out abruptly, but not before the face of the Oretani envoy was shown clear to Dubgetious. Hannibal was behind the envoy and they clasped hands in farewell.

"Convince him we are sincere, Hannibal. We wish the tablet of peace."

"It is past time. My father will be glad to hear the words spoken."

"Until tomorrow."

They parted and Dubgetious stayed locked in hiding, his memory suddenly clear. The envoy was no Oretani. He was a Greek from Sucro and Dubgetious recalled him visiting their village three summers earlier. He remembered how the man had sought him out among the youths too, just to ask him a few simple questions about his mother.

Chapter 18

The Oretani Spears gathered like a mighty river. First came the groups of kin. Men for the most part, but also those women that wielded spears or slings. These merged with others of their clan and in ever greater numbers, raced to heed the unusual summons. The clans joined together on the main trading routes through the territory of the Oretani, all making for the same destination; the war camp of Orissus.

Lyda leaned back on her haunches, staring at the great number of Spears gathered in the large valley chosen by Orissus to hold his army.

"They have come at speed. I feared such a large host would take many more days to gather." She flicked a glance at Tucsux who sat picking at the scabs that had crusted around the dressing on his arm. "You never said how you escaped the Gauls."

The Bastetani warrior shrugged. "When I saw you taken I knew it was a pointless fight and cut my way through their spears."

Cenos, sitting beside him, added, "The Gauls expected us to die meekly. They did not bargain on facing a cornered lynx." She spat a lump of gristle into the wet grass.

"Orissus leads his Spears from here today. He is planning on surprising Hamilcar. I have told him the Gauls are most likely to break." Lyda watched Tucsux carefully and was gladdened when he nodded.

"I think so too. They are hard warriors, but they care more for silver than honour." He looked up at her. "That is not to say they will not fight well."

Lyda said nothing as she stood and shrugged her shoulders to readjust the padded leather armour into a more comfortable position. It was old and brittle, but she could not complain as it had been given as a gift by Orissus.

The others rose, looking to her for direction. She turned slowly, her eyes raking the thousands of Oretani. Still more were converging and soon they would move. She turned to the small company of Bastetani.

"We are just a few and guests of Orissus. Still, it would be wise to be wary of the Oretani in the coming battle. Remain together and do what you must to stay alive, and do not let your guard down."

Cenos, chewing the last of a haunch of sun cured meat, grunted. "We are with you, Lyda. Together we will find Dubgetious and take him home."

The Oretani moved fast. They marched at midday and did not pause until well after dark and then only to eat dry rations and relieve themselves. Lyda and the Bastetani struggled to keep up, their legs and backs aching from the pace so soon after their flight from Hamilcar's army.

The quarter moon set and the cold breeze died away. The thousands of warriors toiling along the rough paths trod for generations into the hills made little sound. Soon after the moon set, the warriors thinned out and settled down under their cloaks to sleep. They had covered much of the distance to the besieged Oretani town. It was unlikely that any enemy scouts would have been roaming the night. When dawn came, they would need to move fast to reach Hamilcar's army before they were spotted.

They rose again just before dawn. Staggering on legs numb from the cold ground, they cursed moodily as they relieved themselves and ate cold rations. As they ate, the Oretani became buoyant at the prospect of the great battle ahead. It was rare for such a host of Spears to gather and they could not see anything but victory before they retired to their villages for the rest of the winter. Lyda and the Bastetani were grim jawed, knowing the enemy and how deadly they were.

A dense mist had risen while they slept, obscuring the valleys and leaving the hilltops exposed to the first coppery rays of sunlight. Oretani horsemen rode out ahead of the marching warriors, intent on silencing Hamilcar's scouts. The clopping of their hooves as they disappeared into the mist quickly became muffled before fading altogether.

The Oretani host moved like a great serpent through the mist filled valley. The only sound they made was the muted tread of leather sandals on rain softened ground. Their war horns hung unused and their battle songs remained sealed behind their lips as they marched to surprise their enemy.

"There!" Cenos was ahead of Lyda and the others and was now pointing at the smudge of campfires beyond the next rise.

"I hear no drums or horns." Tucsux observed.

Lyda hurried forward on stiff legs. The Oretani were gathering on the slopes ahead, keeping a good distance from the ridgeline. She saw Orissus among a group of a hundred horsemen.

"Greetings, Lyda!" He called as she neared. "Hamilcar is making this easy for us."

"No scouts. The gods favour us." She replied, her eyes sliding away to the ridgeline.

"You wish to see?" The Oretani slid from his mount and tossed the reins to an attendant. "Come. There is time as my Spears gather."

He did not slip to his belly as he neared the ridgeline, but strode boldly to the crest of the hill. Lyda stopped beside him and looked down upon the besieging army.

"They are preparing for battle." She hissed before noticing that the enemy lines were formed to face the town rather than the hills from which the Oretani would soon be pouring.

"There are many of them." Orissus grinned as he watched the enemy. "That will only make our victory all the sweeter." His eyes glittered.

Lyda saw a handful of figures emerge from the town. A similar sized group broke from the enemy ranks.

"We must attack at once." Lyda gestured at the delegations.

"Eh? A delegation?" Orissus brushed his fingers through his greased beard. "Perhaps." He mused.

Lyda turned on him, eyes blazing. "If you wish to kill the snake you cut off its head." She stabbed a finger to where the two parties were gathering mid-way between the Carthaginian ranks and the Oretani town walls. "Strike now while Hamilcar is separated from his men. Attack with your horsemen and split him from his army and it will shrivel and die on your spears."

A black frown creased Orissus' brow for a heartbeat. "You have a true warrior heart, Lyda." He smiled thinly as he turned his back on her and called to his leading men, rallying them to him.

The Oretani horsemen flooded down the hillsides to the east of the enemy camp. Four hundred horsemen whipping their sturdy mounts to a fast gallop. Hard on their heels, a thousand spearmen charged.

Lyda stood beside her companions on the ridgeline in the first ranks of the bulk of the Oretani spears and watched as Orissus led the horsemen. The enemy reacted slowly, stunned into gawping inaction.

A hundred warhorns resounded from around her and the massed Oretani surged over the ridgeline, making for the centre of the enemy lines three hundred paces from them.

In a tight cluster among the howling Oretani, Lyda and the Bastetani warriors loped down the hill, making for the campsite of the Gauls. Her hope was that in the past days the Herb Queen had located Dubgetious and could tell her where to find him. If the young woman still lived.

There was a sudden throb of heavy drumming and heartbeats later she saw the enemy lines shift. They were turning to face the onrushing Oretani. Orissus' horsemen were galloping hard at the knot of men in the field outside the town walls. The spearmen following the riders were struck by arrows and spears, but ran on resolutely. Their role was to hold the enemy ranks only as long as it took for the horsemen to run Hamilcar down and kill or capture him.

A great bellowing roar exploded from a hundred throats as the first Oretani warriors clashed with the main army. The impact of shields and blades followed, drumming and ringing across the valley.

Lyda lost sight of Orissus and his horsemen as she reached level ground and her view was blocked by lines of rotting hide tents, lean-tos and mounds of waste. She lifted her shield, seeing the first figures of the enemy ahead of her.

"Lyda!" Tucsux shouted. "On your right!"

She was focused on the loose line of warriors scattered among the tents and wagons. Turning at Tucsux warning, she saw another group of warriors gathered behind a large wagon. They were twenty paces away and crouched low. Seeing they had been noticed, they let loose a shrill war cry and lifted their bows, bringing the nocked arrows to bear on her and the Bastetani warriors.

She hissed and dropped to a knee, lifting her round shield to cover her chest and ducking her head. The enemy archers let loose their arrows which whipped towards her. An arrow slammed into her shield, sending a jolt through her shoulder while another hissed past her forehead. A solid impact behind her signalled a hit and the body of a warrior crashed to the ground almost on her heels. She gasped and turned, fearing it was Tucsux that had been struck. It was a Bastetani warrior from her village, but not the hard warrior she had fought so often beside. The man's eyes were wide, blinking furiously. The feathered end of an arrow protruded from his throat, its barbed end buried in the dirt at his neck. Frothing blood welled from his mouth and gushed through his beard. His blinking ceased and he stared with unseeing eyes at the sky. Fearsome battle rage consumed her and she howled her war cry.

Springing forward, she raced towards the group of archers, her spear held underhand, ready to tear into the enemy. Her fellow warriors were beside her, their bellows deafening. The archers were nocking arrows, hands shaking. A youth with not a hair on his face, fumbled his arrow, dropping it at his feet. Beside him, a graybeard cursed the boy and lifted his bow, arrow nocked. The graybeard aimed it at Lyda and released.

In the next instant, she was in his face, her spear buried deep in his gut. His arrow had split the skin under her shoulder and passed on to bury itself in the shield of the warrior at her back. Lyda twisted the spear and punched her shield into the graybeard, driving him off the spear which tore from his body, releasing a gush of warm fluid that splattered her legs and filled her sandals.

The archers broke, the youth leading the retreat, his bow left lying in the mud, arrows scattered.

Panting hard, Lyda pulled up and called to her warriors to hold although none were keen to chase the archers into the maze of tents.

Tucsux hurled a spear overhand, sending it spinning through the smoke-filled air into the back of the rearmost archer. He growled and kicked a dying man in the jaw, sending blood and teeth splattering across the ground.

"Tucsux! We make for the Gaul's camp." Lyda shouted, bringing the battle mad warrior around.

He flexed his fists and took a breath. Oretani warriors were rampaging through the lines of tents, howling like shades released from the dark. There was a deeper hum of battle raging to their right, beyond the tent lines where the main fighting forces had met.

Cenos appeared, blood covering her face, her left ear ragged and bleeding down her neck. Despite the wound, she was grinning.

"Felt good gutting them!" She raised her bloodied spear high and whooped.

Lyda grinned back and nodded. "The Gauls will be harder to kill."

Cenos' smile only widened. "They will die today same as they did when they tried to kill us in the dark."

They jogged steadily through the lines of abandoned tents, making for the Gaul's tents. It was likely that many of the Gauls would be in the lines of Hamilcar's army, fighting for their lives against Orissus' many Spears. There would be others that remained to guard their possessions though. Lyda invoked her gods, praying that the Herb Queen was still alive. That Dubgetious was safe.

A spear cleaved into a Bastetani on her far left, thrown by a warrior perched on an overturned wagon. Lyda growled and hurled her own spear and saw it bite deep into the man's thigh. Two more spears thudded into him, throwing him from the wagon.

"That was an Oretani warrior!" Cenos snarled.

Lyda drew her sword, a poor thing, pitted with rust. Also a gift from Orissus. As she did, a band of Oretani charged from beyond the wagon, screaming their war cries and hurling their spears.

The Bastetani batted at the spears with their shields, knocking them aside. They then charged with Tucsux leading the way. The warrior had grabbed up a discarded spear and had it balanced at his side.

The Oretani charging them were of the worst kind. Wearing simple uncured skins, their hair knotted with bones and skin daubed with coloured clay, they were little more than the savage hill warriors who held scant regard for honour or oath.

Tascux punched his spear into the first's face, taking off his jaw and dropping him thrashing to the ground. Then Cenos was amongst them, her powerful shoulders absorbing impacts against her shield while driving her spear into warm flesh.

Lyda, growling and spitting, struck. A wiry woman hacked at her with a metal tipped club. Lyda swayed beneath the swipe and plunged her blade into the woman's gut below her naval. Whipping the blade out, she kicked the staggering woman in the knee and opened her neck as she fell. The fight lasted no more than a dozen heartbeats. A frenzy of stabbing and screaming. The Bastetani were reduced to eight men and women. The band of Oretani lay dead.

"Many more like them and we will not survive to fight the Gauls." Cenos gasped, her face white.

Tucsux took her arm and helped her to stand upright. Fresh blood glistened on her tunic, a raw wound gaping below her breast.

Lyda, an immeasurable sadness heavy on her soul, wiped her sword clean and sheathed it. Taking up a spear from a dead companion, she tapped the head to test its strength.

"The Gauls' camp is along the line. Stay in the thickest of the smoke and try to avoid any more beasts like these."

Chapter 19

The morning dawned fresh, with a bright sun warming the tired camp and lancing golden rays through the smoke from a hundred campfires. Already, the army was up; the warriors filled with a sense of impending victory.

Dubgetious, revitalised after a few hours of sleep once he had been relieved of sentry duty, spent time honing and polishing his sword. His tent mates eyed the heavy blade and grinned at his efforts.

"It looks like a pregnant adder." A wiry warrior quipped.

"Bites like one too." Dubgetious threw back. "Want to feel?"

Men laughed and nodded, spitting on their own blades and polishing them to a shine. A bellow from down the line got their attention and they sprang to their feet.

Amma, their leading man, was striding up the line of tents, slapping them with a gnarled stave, showering the occupants with the heavy dew that hung from the hides.

"Looks like something is happening at last." Dubgetious remarked.

"Get your armour on and form lines!" Amma called. "Today we take that cursed town!"

Cheers grew as the news travelled and warriors poured onto the fields around the town walls. Dubgetious found himself and his tent mates lined up facing the town gates some two hundred paces away. Men joked and laughed, their eyes wide and lips dry. Dubgetious saw men touching amulets and invoking their gods. Spotting a mound of rocks lifted from the fields by Oretani farmers in seasons past, Dubgetious climbed to the top to get a look over the heads of his fellows. The army formed a crescent moon of blades facing the town. The Libyans occupied the centre. Gauls held the west flank and Turdetani the east. A forest of spears swayed above a carpet of polished chest plates and helmets.

A ripple of movement proceeded from the Carthaginian pavilion and presently he saw Hamilcar striding through the lines of warriors, a handful of leading men keeping pace with him.

The Carthaginian general strolled casually to the front of his army and stopped to stare at the gates of the Oretani town. The squeal of wood and grinding of the gates dragging over the rocky road rose as they were hauled open. Four men walked slowly through the gates and stopped to stare at the massed army. Two servants rushed past them carrying benches which they set equidistant between the town and Hamilcar's army. The men walked slowly forward to stop beside the benches. They wore tunics and cloaks. No blades among them, nor armour of any kind. The warriors around Dubgetious groaned and cursed, knowing now that it would be a long morning of waiting in lines as Hamilcar thrashed out a treaty with the town elders. There would be no looting and plunder this day.

Hamilcar took his time exchanging pleasantries with warriors down the line. The Carthaginian ignored the waiting delegation and came closer, smiling and laughing with his men. He looked up, just paces from where Dubgetious stood elevated above the other warriors. The burly general grinned at him.

"Greetings, young Bastetani! How look our Oretani friends? Anxious no doubt!" He laughed confidently and finally turned and made his way to the waiting delegation followed by three leading Carthaginian advisors.

Dubgetious yawned and turned on the rocks, taking in the low hills surrounding the town and valley in which Hamilcar had set his besieging army. A band of Masulians came thundering over a low hill to the east, no doubt expecting battle and arriving in haste. Their numbers swelled until half a thousand riders were in sight.

He had to squint into the early morning light to make out the horsemen more clearly. The leading riders passed through shade cast by towering pines on a far hill and Dubgetious' brow creased with confusion. They did not have the look of Masulians. Their horses were larger, their spears longer. As they neared, he heard their shouts and cold certainty struck him.

"We are attacked!" He yelled, pointing. Others were watching the horsemen with bored curiosity. The riders' numbers were insignificant in the face of Hamilcar's army and so were dismissed as unthreatening.

"Fool! They are Masulians. No enemy, so outnumbered would attack." Came the general response.

Dubgetious leaped from the rocks and grabbed at Amma who stood silent and alert.

"They are attacking! Not us, but Hamilcar!" Dubgetious pointed at their exposed general in the centre of the cleared field.

"The bastards! You are right!" The Libyan cursed and shouted for the drums to beat the alarm.

"Look!" Dubgetious cried. Warriors now surged from the hills, running behind the riders. A thousand at least. Still the Punic drums remained silent.

The horsemen swept off the hills and galloped hard across the face of the startled Turdetani warriors on the right flank. Amma growled with frustration.

"The fools do nothing but stand and watch!" He spun on his heel and drew his sword. Raising it, he bellowed at the top of his voice for his warriors to step forward. "You too, Dubgetious."

Dubgetious joined the lines of Libyans who began to advance towards their general. The advance was uneven though, with the warriors on the far flanks taken by surprise and hurrying to catch up and straighten the ranks.

The horsemen closed the distance to Hamilcar who was now standing and gesturing angrily with his arm towards the oncoming riders. Dubgetious could hear the yells of the riders and feel the vibrations of their galloping horses through the soles of his sandals. He doubted very much that they would be in time to head off the horsemen. Was this the treason Amma had warned him of? Was this what Hannibal and the man from Sucro had been plotting? Dubgetious shook his head. No, they had mentioned the tablet of peace. This was not the work of a son such as Hannibal.

"We are too slow!" He grumbled.

"Stay in line. This is no time to rush like hounds to bitches." An older warrior advised him sternly.

The Turdetani had finally roused themselves, but already the enemy riders were beyond them. The following spearmen were not though and the ranks of levied Turdetani surged towards these.

Shouted commands and curses reached Dubgetious and he snatched a look over his shoulder to see a party of Carthaginian horsemen pushing their way through the Libyan ranks. He recognised the foremost rider. Hannibal, Hamilcar's son. The Carthaginian had five riders with him, two Carthaginians and three Masulians. They slapped their spears at the warriors blocking their path, cursing them and knocking them aside with their mounts. Hannibal's horse baulked when a drummer belatedly began to beat the advance from nearby. As Dubgetious gasped, the horse reared wildly. Hannibal's eyes locked with his as the mount rose high on its rear legs and twisted. Then the Carthaginian toppled from its back and the horse crashed into the press of Libyan warriors. There were cries of dismay and hoarse shouts of anger. A second horse bolted, unseating its Carthaginian rider and breaking through the confused warriors. It staggered paces away from Dubgetious, a hoof fouled on a warrior who had fallen under it. It was all the opportunity Dubgetious needed. He shoved two men from his path, using all the strength in his wide shoulders, and grabbed the mount's trailing reins close to its muzzle. He leaped, sending his right leg over its back and pulling himself awkwardly astride while still holding his spear in his right hand. Amma saw him and opened his mouth to remonstrate, but after a quick glance at the closing horsemen, he nodded and shouted. "Go, Dubgetious! Ride like a djin!" The old warrior pushed aside his men, opening a gap through the lead ranks.

Dubgetious rucked his heels hard across the mount's ribs and yelled. It screamed and leaped forward, tearing through the gap and out into the field ahead of the Libyans. Into the path of the oncoming enemy riders. Dubgetious hauled on the reins and cursed to see the enemy so close already. He noticed a flash of movement from the corner of his eye and looking, saw the three Masulian riders were with him, their horsemanship had proved better than that of the Carthaginians. Dubgetious nodded nervously at the Masulians who grinned and whooped, shaking their spears at the enemy riders.

Hamilcar was running towards them, his face red with exertion. Dubgetious leaned low over the mount's withers, trying to coax every bit of speed from it. His ears filled with the roar of a thousand hooves striking the ground. The Masulians edged to his right, forming a screen between him and the onrushing enemy riders whose mouths gaped and eyes burned with fury. They were Oretani.

Dubgetious brought the horse to a halt, dragging its head around to the left and almost knocking Hamilcar from his feet. A roaring crash brought his head around and his eyes widened in shock. Thousands upon thousands of enemy warriors were surging down the hills to the rear of the Carthaginian army. In places, they were already driving their spears into the ranks of surprised warriors.

Dubgetious felt Hamilcar's hand grip his thigh as the general made to leap astride the mount behind him.

"No, you must ride alone. It has not the wind to carry us both away." Dubgetious slipped from the horse and handed the reins to Hamilcar.

The man stared hard at Dubgetious. "You would die to save me?"

"I will find another way." Dubgetious knelt and allowed Hamilcar to use his shoulder as a step to mount.

The Carthaginian general turned the mount in a tight circle. The enemy riders were already between him and his army. With a grunt of annoyance, he raked his heels across the mount's withers and faced to the west where he could perhaps still circle around to reach his men. As he rode away, he shouted back over his shoulder.

"Try to stay alive, young Bastetani, for I would like to reward you greatly!"

Dubgetious stood rooted to the spot as the rest of the Carthaginian delegation ran past him, their eyes round with fear. The Masulian riders were circling past the very noses of the enemy riders, hurling their light throwing spears as they ululated. The enemy riders roared in fury as Hamilcar rode away and turned their horses after him. Others rode at the Masulians, eager to swat them and their deadly spears down. The panting delegates were the first to fall. The horsemen whooped as they ran them down, cutting them across the shoulders and bringing screams of pain and terror from their throats. They circled and let the weary men run on before coming back to slice at their buttocks, drawing great lines of red in their flesh. A man tripped and fell to jeers from the Oretani. Two riders slipped from their horses and bound the gibbering Carthaginian's ankles. Remounting, they dragged him after them.

Dubgetious went to a knee and lifted his spear. The horsemen were almost upon him and he wanted to die quickly rather than be flayed alive. A group of the riders came at him, their lips twisted with hatred and intent.

The trio of Masulians swooped past them, shrieking like shades released from the lands of death, raining spears into the riders. Men screamed and fell. Spears flew between the two groups and a Masulian took a broad-bladed spear in his forehead. He dropped amongst the flashing hooves without a sound. Dubgetious snarled as an Oretani rider emerged from the melee, his eyes on the Masulians who rode rings around them. A light throwing spear bounced and quivered from his shoulder. Dubgetious surged forward from the ground, shoving his spear up into the distracted warrior's body and lifting him from the horse. Releasing the spear, Dubgetious snatched for the reins and missed. The horse, maddened by the panic of its now dead rider, the coppery stink of blood and the screams of its fellows, spun away from Dubgetious and launched a kick at his head. He ducked under the flailing hoofs and dived, landing beside the dangling reins. Grasping, his fist closed around the coarse leather reins and he allowed the mount to pull him to his feet. In a heartbeat, he was astride, pressing his knees hard into its shoulders, he held tight as it turned in a close circle, neighing and snapping at him. Then he flicked the reins and let it run.

Chapter 20

Lyda and the remnants of the small Bastetani force, stole through the chaotic camp. Seeking the densest smoke, always avoiding ravaging bands of Oretani warriors or hard fighting Libyans and Turdetani. Of the Gauls, there seemed to be no sign.

"The Gaul's lines were near here I think." Tucsux growled, sniffing the air and pointing to a cluster of burning wagons. "I recognise those three wagons. They were damaged and to be repaired."

"Which way from here?" Lyda scanned about her warily. The battle was moving their way and groups of warriors were running in every direction, some feverishly seeking loot, others to merely survive.

Tucsux said nothing, but moved forward purposefully. Lyda nodded after him and the rest followed, eyes darting everywhere, knuckles white. Cenos brought up the rear, face pale and brow sweat soaked. Lyda took her arm and helped her forward.

"Be good to see that bloody Herb Queen." Cenos croaked, through her panting.

"Keep your breath for walking. She will be close."

The Gauls, when they appeared, were moving fast. They came from the north, bloodied and missing many of their number, but they moved with purpose. Lyda saw them first and whistled the alarm. At once, the Bastetani warriors folded themselves behind any available cover. Lyda dragged Cenos behind a butchered mule, crouching in the bloody mud and leaning close to the creatures stinking belly.

The Gauls, silent for once, padded on, unaware of the Bastetani. Tucsux raised a hand and Lyda and the rest rose to follow. A murmur caught Lyda's attention. It had sounded as though a shade had called her name. The hair on her arms stood and an icy shiver swept down her spine. It came again, more clearly in a fortuitous lull in the sounds of battle. With a soft whistle to alert Tucsux, she turned to the sound.

The Herb Queen lay beneath an overturned wagon, her face bruised and swollen, eyes almost shut with blood that had streamed from the vicious cut to her head. Lyda gasped at the sight and dropped to her knees to hold the young woman's hand.

"What has happened?" She asked softly.

The Herb Queen grinned through split lips showing blood between her teeth. "War." She hawked and spat a glob of blood weakly from her mouth. "Water if you have."

Cenos uncapped her waterskin and held it to the woman's lips. "And I was hoping you would be mending me." Her voice was gentle.

The Herb Queen drank, choked and pushed the skin away. "Get this cursed wagon off my leg and I would." She grinned again and Lyda saw a spark in her eye.

"You are not dying?" Her relief was overwhelming.

"Not today. Horsemen did this as I ran." She touched her wounded head gingerly. "The wagon turned and fell on me after, saving me from worse." Her grin flashed again. "Your son passed. Riding like he had a fire burning in his sack." She grabbed at Lyda's wrist. "Lyda, he was following the Barca. You should think about what that means."

Lyda's exultant expression faltered and crimson blooms grew on her cheeks. The warrior woman visibly shuddered and lifted her face to the heavens from which rained soot and burning embers.

"I will do what needs doing." She ground out.

Tucsux and four more Bastetani cursed and strained to heave the wagon up. Lyda and Cenos grabbed the Herb Queen beneath her arms and hauled her from under the wagon when it lifted. She writhed silently for a heartbeat as blood gushed back into her leg, her fingers clutching her knee.

"Broken?"

"The gods have other plans. It will be fine." She grimaced and cursed as a cramp seized the muscles of her leg. Catching her breath, she went on. "You can still find him, Lyda. He went past not long before you showed." She pointed. "Ride towards the bald rock on the face of that hill."

Lyda stood and squinted, seeing the rock in the distance. She also saw the horsemen. Just two of them, tiny as fleas, riding swiftly across the face of the hill.

"We have no mounts!" She cursed.

"Their own will be winded. If we follow we will catch up to them." Cenos grunted, standing resolutely.

Tucsux nodded, eyes fixed on Lyda. She smiled then, a hard smile.

Dubgetious beat down a warrior hauling at his leg, smashing his blade against the man's iron helmet and splitting it. Another thrust a spear at his belly, forcing him to jerk his knee into the shaft, deflecting the blade. He lashed a backhanded blow across that man's face, slicing him from ear to ear. Then he was free, the last of the Oretani warriors behind him. Ahead, rode Hamilcar. The General clung to his horse as it laboured up a hillside.

Dubgetious' own mount was breathing hard, its coat lathered white, but he urged it on remorselessly. He could not let Hamilcar die. The man was responsible for what had happened to his clan, to Beratza, but Dubgetious knew that if Hamilcar died and Hasdrubal came seeking revenge, the hills would be drenched in the blood of his people. He had also seen the sophistication of the Carthaginians and knew that nothing would be the same for the Bastetani, Turdetani or any of the people of his land. Hamilcar and Carthage offered a new world for them all.

Hamilcar pitched from his mount and tumbled through the wiry brush that coated the hillside, arms flopping loosely.

When Dubgetious reached him, the general was pulling himself up, blood trickling from the corner of his mouth. He leapt from his mount which promptly skittered away, determined to run free.

"We are lost. How did this happen?" Hamilcar was staring at the valley below. The Oretani held the greatest swath. They had overrun the entire camp where they howled and looted still. Thousands of Hamilcar's warriors were retreating south, abandoning the field to the enemy. The rest lay mauled and dead where they had been killed fighting or slain as they tried to flee.

"The gods willed it. Your army is still strong. We just need to reach it."

"My sons. Hannibal. He must live." With these words, Hamilcar rallied and his eyes lost the blank look of despair. He clutched Dubgetious' shoulder and rose ponderously.

Dubgetious helped him stand, seeing only now the fletching of an arrow standing proud in the Carthaginian's lower back. It looked to be a deep wound. The kind that would kill in a day. He lifted Hamilcar's arm over his shoulder and pulled him up the hillside. Even with his broad shoulders and the strength of his youth, he was gasping by the time he reached the crest of the hill.

"Lower me. I must drink." Hamilcar muttered through his bedraggled beard.

Gratefully, Dubgetious set him down. As he did so, he saw a line of warriors loping towards the foot of the hill. His heart missed a beat and he cursed. The Oretani would run all night to capture Hamilcar.

"They are hunting us. We cannot stay here."

Hamilcar had seen the enemy as well and spat. "Bastards. I do not even have so much as an eating knife."

A second group of warriors was now racing towards the hill. It would soon be swarming with enemy blades.

"The hill slopes down to the river beyond. There will be places to conceal ourselves." Dubgetious lifted Hamilcar once again, the sweat from the ascent still not dried.

They lurched over the hill and began the painful path down. Thorn bushes lashed at their legs and arms, rocks and roots caught their ankles and mud set them sliding painfully across rough rocks. Pace by shuffling pace, the two managed to worm their way deeper into the dense growth above the river. Dubgetious could already hear the calls of the hunters from the top of the hill. They had no hounds, but the trail would be easy enough to find.

They stumbled from beneath a dense growth of bushes onto a rocky promontory overlooking the river raging below them. The rains had filled it from bank to bank with a torrent of mud-brown water.

"The gods are not done with us yet, it seems." Hamilcar coughed a fine spray of red from his lips, groaned and slid to the ground.

Dubgetious paced nervously and peered through the thick foliage back the way they had come. He could hear nothing over the roaring waters and his heart sank when he spied a shadowy form moving through the dense growth. Another followed and as his eyes adjusted to the gloom beneath the canopy of trees and brush, he saw still more.

"They have found us." He whispered, dragging his sword from its sheath.

The Carthaginian nodded, his eyes flicking between the blade and him. "It is over for me then. It would be a favour if you would allow me to use that blade to deny them taking me captive."

Dubgetious' chin dipped. "If it comes to that I will." His smile, made crooked by his nerves, lifted his lips. "They are not so many yet."

Hamilcar grinned and looked away. "I was young and brave too once." He turned back, his face sorrowful. "I release you from your oath. Go now before they kill you too."

Dubgetious frowned, uncertain. "It would be wrong."
Hamilcar struggled to his feet, his face grim. "Enough of honour and bravery! Take this chance to live!" He reached out his hand, fingers dark with blood and dirt, for the sword Dubgetious held and then his eyes flicked beyond Dubgetious.
Whirling on his heel, sword lifted to strike, Dubgetious growled and then gaped at the warriors breaking from the cover of the bush to stand before him.

"Mother?" His eyes grew wide, his chin trembled, as though a boy again.

"Son." Voice thick with tender emotion, her face a pattern of dirt and blood, Lyda stepped out of the shadows.
At her back were Tucsux and Cenos. Another figure lingered in the gloom and Dubgetious guessed it was Eppa.

Lyda's lips twisted as she glared at the Carthaginian standing stooped and bloody a pace behind Dubgetious. "The Barca?"
Dubgetious held his sword stiffly at his side. "Hamilcar of Carthage."
Lyda stepped forward, her intent clear in narrowed eyes and clenched jaw.

Dubgetious blocked her. "I swore an oath to Hamilcar. Do not force me to break it or…" He pushed weakly with his left hand at Lyda's chest.
His mother leaned against his outstretched hand, her spear held cocked at her shoulder. "He slaughtered our people. Took you as a slave!" Veins swelled at her throat.

"You were not there, Mother!" His eyes went to Tucsux standing at Lyda's shoulder. "We fought and lost. All our clan would have perished if I had not given my oath. You would have surely done the same?"

Tucsux moved fast, his hand a blur, slamming his spear down across Dubgetious' wrist. Dubgetious saw the old warrior's move coming and caught the blow with his blade with an ear-splitting ring of iron on iron. Tucsux' spear head snapped, a wicked edge spinning away into the river.

Dubgetious snarled and struck, shearing the shaft of the spear just above Tucsux hand. Lyda swept out a foot and kicked his knee, folding his leg under him. In a heartbeat, she was standing over him, nostrils flared in fury.

"Do you know how many of my companions have died searching for you? Yet here you are defending him." She choked, gasping as tears welled in her eyes. "I killed Venza for allowing you to be taken."

"You killed my father?" He gasped.

"He was not…" Lyda snapped a look over her shoulder at a sudden scream from within the trees.

"I honour my oath." Dubgetious took the opportunity to twist and draw his short knife, ready to strike.

"I offered to free him of his oath. Your son is a good man." Hamilcar tried to stand straight, but his legs tottered. "Curses. I am a dead man, anyway. Kill me and take your son home."

The thumping impact of a spear strike silenced them all for a heartbeat. A heavy spear was lodged deep in the chest of the veteran Bastetani warrior. Tucsux glared down at the shaft for a dying heartbeat before looking up at Lyda.

"The truth. He deserves it, Lyda." The warrior toppled to the ground, his shade already free of his dead body.

The scene erupted into a frenzied rush of warriors and blades. Wild war cries shrilled from the trees and another spear hurtled into the clearing, narrowly missing both Dubgetious and a stricken Lyda.

"Mother! I will fight them! Take Hamilcar down the river."
He caught her arm and turned her away from the lifeless body
of her long-time shield brother.

Cenos growled a war cry and hacked at the first of the enemy
to spring from the trees, taking him above the knee. He
shrieked and folded onto the rocks at her feet, hands clutching
the splintered limb. With a grunt, Cenos shoved him into the
roaring river below them.

Dubgetious shook his mother who lifted her arms, loosening
his grip on her. She slapped him across the cheek and then
embraced him for a fleeting moment, savouring the life of her
only child deeply.

"I must stay. The world now belongs to those like you who
can build new bridges."

The trees shook as unseen warriors leaped down the hill to
reach them on the promontory.

Cenos backed up, sweat blinding her eyes, shoulders hunched.
Dubgetious made to protest, but Cenos cursed him.

"You deaf, pup? Your mother and I are dead. Take your king
and go build us a bloody great pyre. Do it now!" She ducked as
three warriors leaped from the trees. Her spear a flash of
motion that opened a man's thigh from knee to groin and
drenched her in his blood.

Dubgetious was shoved back by his mother who leaped at their
attackers. Her war cry as piercing as flint, her sword bit sharp
and claimed another.

Cenos spun away from a blow that opened her throat, her eyes
boring into Dubgetious' own. Blood flowing in a sheet from
the wound, she raised a hand and pointed Dubgetious to the
far bank. An Oretani warrior drove his spear into Cenos' back
before she had bled dry, its wicked blade opening her chest,
splitting her tunic and mutilating a breast.

Lyda flew at the warrior, only to be beaten back by two more
who appeared from among the trees. A club slammed into her
elbow and bones snapped like dried twigs.

Hamilcar placed heavy hands on Dubgetious' shoulders,
holding him back though it cost him deeply.

"Do not watch, boy."

"Go Dubgetious!" Lyda screamed as her blade lashed out, cutting through the clubman's ankle.

Dubgetious saw another figure materialise from the shadows. The warrior from Sucro. He was bloody and soiled, chest sucking in great bellows of air as he shouldered through the ever-growing numbers of Oretani warriors. Dubgetious knew him as a man of his mother's people to the east. The Greek saw Lyda at the feet of her killers and his face turned the colour of winter cloud. He looked past her bloodied body and straight at Dubgetious. The warrior from Sucro reached out a hand to him and at that moment, Hamilcar dragged him from the rock and into a void.

Epilogue

Clouds the colour of newly forged iron helmets grew thick, blotting out the sun and a cold wind gusted through the valley, whipping rust coloured foam from the river into thick drifts between boulders and bleached timber. The scent of river, rock and rain was thick and the roar of the cataracts was shadowed by the rush of wind through forests that reached down to the river.

Dubgetious worked his hand into a crevasse and bunched it into a fist. He felt the pressure on his knuckles when he pulled, but no pain. With his other hand, he gripped tight the thick wool of the general's tunic where it bulged from his armour. With a long deep growl, he heaved and pulled himself higher, feeling the wind whipping his legs now as they came clear of the river's icy grip.

He lay his head down and breathed deeply until the white clouds passed from his vision and he could see straight once more. It took him a long while to drag himself and the motionless general from the ever-rushing water and when at last he rolled onto a moss-covered rock above the water's edge; he had all the strength of a newly hatched duckling. He closed his eyes, overwhelmed by a weariness that fed on his mind like a malign shade. He dared not sleep though. His flesh had turned the colour of the clouds above and he shook violently. He would never wake if he slept.

Crawling to his feet against a boulder, he looked to the dark forest, first for danger and then for shelter. He dragged the general into the tree line and then used the last of his strength to strike a spark which he fed the shredded inside of tree bark.

As the flames grew, Dubgetious risked adding branches more green than seasoned. The wind would whip the smoke away into the forest where no man would know its source. He was wrong.

He slept beyond where dreams catch the spirit. There in the deepest dark where no sound or scent floats.

He came awake when the first blow landed, snapping his head to the side and splitting the skin above his eye so that he was blinded by blood.

"Tie him I ordered! Not kill him." The voice cracked through the clouds that obscured Dubgetious' vision. He shook his head and snarled as knees dropped onto his arms and thighs, pinning him. Calloused hands tightened their hold. The hands of old warriors.

"I serve the Barca! Release me!" He cursed wildly, jerking his arms and thrashing with his legs to unbalance the man that pinned his thighs.

One of the warriors spat in his face. "Best get on your knees then. The son of the man you killed is here."

"Which man would that be?" Dubgetious ripped a hand free and struck the warrior across the ear, sending him rolling.

Dubgetious twisted and kicked free of the second warrior and hurled a handful of dirt and pine needles at his face. Springing to his feet, he came to an abrupt halt.

Hannibal, son of Hamilcar Barca was kneeling beside the stiffened body of his father. Slowly the young Carthaginian ran a hand over the stub of an arrow that protruded from Hamilcar's back. "This was not your kill. I know this Dubgetious of the Bastetani. Yet, here you are, alone with the body of Carthage's greatest general. My father." The voice was that of Hamilcar's son, the tone was that of a man with ice in his veins and fire in his gut. Hannibal nodded at a grim-faced warrior.

Dubgetious tensed, but the warrior tossed an object to him. It landed at his feet and he blinked at it. His falcata, secure in its scabbard, now swollen with river water and splitting at every stitch.

"The sword over which you took an oath to fight for and protect our general."

Dubgetious nodded. "An oath I held to." He saw his mother's face. "An oath I stood by." He heard Tucsux deep voice. "An oath I failed." Saw Cenos mouthing her last words. "I laid his body there. The body of Hamilcar Barca whom I dragged from the river."

There was silence. The warriors around him stood like rocks, hands gripping their blades.

Hannibal rose and faced him. "Dubgetious of the Bastetani, where is the cloak I gave you?"

"Like as not, wrapped about the shoulders of some bastard Oretani." Dubgetious eyed Hannibal's cloak. "Mine?"

Hannibal's lips moved, but no smile grew. He threw a handful of sticks onto the embers of Dubgetious' fire, stirred them and gave them air until they burned. "Bring the others. We camp here." He turned dark eyes on Dubgetious. "You fought at my father's side to the last?"

Dubgetious shrugged. "I saw you fall from your mount and I managed to get to Hamilcar before the enemy reached him. It was by fortune I could follow him from the battlefield." He shuffled closer to the fire, his eyes smarting from the smoke, but eager for the warmth. "He was struck by an arrow at some point. I helped him beyond the hills and hoped to rejoin the army which was within sight, but on the wrong side of the enemy."

Hannibal prodded the fire with a stick, eyes distant. "We retreated south, but when I heard my father was unaccounted for, I forced Eshmun and Abdmelqart to make a stand." The young Carthaginian held a smile for just a blink of an eye. "The Oretani did not like that, but by then they had no more surprises for us." He looked hard at Dubgetious. "There is a look in your eye that speaks of more pain than is justified by the death of Hamilcar Barca."

Dubgetious rubbed his face, smearing new ash into skin washed pale by the river. He thought of the warrior from Sucro and his shock at seeing Lyda killed. Dubgetious sensed a dark truth in the man's reaction.

Hannibal grunted into the long silence that followed. "We found a woman." He shook his head. "A Bastetani."

Barely hearing, Dubgetious saw his mother in his mind's eye. Her long seasons away from home. Her restiveness through the winters confined to their village and land. His eyes trailed the sparks rising from the fire into the forest canopy.

"My mother. She was not with us when your father took our village. She came after me." Dubgetious felt his throat tightened. "Her wish was to end Hamilcar's life." He picked the broken stitching from the scabbard. "I defied her and then saw her die. That was when I fled with Hamilcar into the river."

Hannibal nodded, his eyes bright. He lifted his hand and extended it to Dubgetious. "You defied your mother for the life of my father, your people's enemy?" Hannibal croaked, overcome with emotion. "Did you kill her too?"

Dubgetious' hands shook. "I would not have been able to do that. Even on an oath." He dropped his chin to his chest.

"There are few with honour as steadfast as yours, Dubgetious of the Bastetani. I will see that you and your clan are rewarded handsomely."

Dubgetious smiled and gripped Hannibal's arm in return. "No more war between us would be a good start. Like all good things though, very difficult to make real."

Hannibal barked a laugh. "Ha! Spoken like a Greek." He fell silent and released Dubgetious' arm.

Dubgetious watched Hannibal's eyes flick to the outlines of warriors carrying torches through the forest. The Carthaginian looked uncomfortable and for a moment he wondered what it was that Hannibal was thinking. His eyes narrowed with a sudden apprehension. "You said you found a woman?" He turned to peer at the approaching figures and then spun back to Hannibal who nodded.

"Yes. My healers have treated her as best they could, but…" He held his hands out, palms up. "She speaks your tongue and has said your name many times."

Dubgetious rose slowly to his feet, seeing 'Renza fall and her lingering death. Cenos hacked and bled dry. His mother's brutal killing. There had been another figure in the shadows before the Oretani attacked. Eppa? Why then call his name as she lay dying?

Two men stepped from the trees, carrying between them a litter on which lay a ragged mess of furs and linen, dyed red and ochre. The bundle quivered, and a hand slipped from under the covering so that its bloodied nails dragged through the carpet of pine needles. Dubgetious halted the pair of servants with a gesture and lifted away a length of linen to stare at what lay beneath.

Not Lyda nor Cenos nor any other warrior woman. The woman Hannibal's scouts had found was another. He pressed his palm to her cheek made round and discoloured by swelling and then traced a finger along the swirls of inked scars at her brow.

"Herb Queen."

His words were a faint whisper, but her eyelids fluttered and opened. For a long moment she gazed at him through eyes dulled by pain. A tear formed at the corner of her eye and Dubgetious lifted it to his lips.

"The pup is gone, I see." Her voice was ragged, but firm. Her hands closed on his forearm. "I see instead a warrior and a man."

Dubgetious, smelled her blood and tasted her salty tear. "Will you live?"

She closed her eyes and inhaled deeply, wincing. "The Oretani blade bit deep, but I will heal."

"Who is the warrior from Sucro?" His voice was heavy with dread.

Her eyelids lifted and her gaze burned into him. "The brother of a king. The brother of your true father."

Dubgetious clenched his teeth and nodded. "Did Venza know?"

The Herb Queen shook her head and coughed. A warm hand came to rest on his shoulder as Hannibal stepped to his side.

"She needs to heal. Come away and let her rest."

Dubgetious pulled the matted furs to her chin. "Yes, there is a great need for healing." He turned to Hannibal. "Will your army continue as it has?"

The young Carthaginian dipped his chin. "Tanit has guided this Herb Queen here to where you and I stand by the body of my father. Is this not a sign? A sign that it is a time to heal?" He smiled solemnly. "I am no General, Dubgetious, but I promise I will do all I can to carve a tablet of peace between our peoples."

The End

Brief Historical Note

When Hamilcar Barca of Carthage invaded Iberia in 237BC, he used his veteran Libyan and Numidian mercenaries to crush the proud Turdetani tribe in the south around the modern day city of Cadiz.

Keen to lay his hands on the rich silver deposits in the mountains we know today as the Sierra Morena, he turned his eyes north and west, subjugating clans and levying their warriors into his mercenary army. Not without battle though, for the Turdetani were a fiercely proud and wealthy people. Istolatios of the Turdetani resisted with help from other tribes, but was quickly defeated and part of his army incorporated into Hamilcar's own. Indortes of the Turdetani then raised 50,000 Spears to challenge Hamilcar. Mismatched in every way, they folded and fled Hamilcar's veteran army of ruthless warriors and war elephants. Frustrated with the continued resistance from the Turdetani, Hamilcar made Indortes' death an agonizing one, first torturing and then crucifying him. No doubt, he meant for the Iberians would take the message to heart.

Within two years, Turdetania was thoroughly subdued with the best of their warriors dead or forced to fight as levies for Hamilcar.

The Turdetani were just the first of the Iberian people to feel the weight of the conqueror's heel on their necks. The smaller Turduli were swept up and then the western Bastetani and southern Oretani.

From 235 to 231BC, Hamilcar expanded his dominance east. Brave and resolute, the Iberians contested the expansion hotly. Grudges between clans and tribes were put aside as the Iberians allied themselves against the deadly invader.
Hamilcar's forces were blunt instruments of destruction and they even antagonized the Bastetani enough to make this usually peaceful tribe take up their spears and fight.

Rise of the Spears is set in the year 228BC, and follows Hamilcar leading his forces north-west and deep into the heart of the Oretani lands. This would be the great Carthaginian general's last campaign for the father of Hannibal Barca would perish in the autumn, the manner of his death changing from one source to the next. The consensus seems to point to a battle in which Hamilcar was slain or drowned.
The main character in Rise of the Spears, Dubgetious, is fictitious, but he speaks for all those unwilling levies forced to fight in Hamilcar's army.

The story is a prequel to the Sons of Iberia series which covers the 2nd Punic War fought between Carthage and Rome. Dubgetious features in the 3rd title in the series, Gladius Winter.

Also by J. Glenn Bauer

Sons of Iberia:
Warhorn
Maharra
Gladius Winter

The Runeovex Secret

Von Steiner's Gold
(Written with T. J. Hobson)

About Myself

As a child, my playground was the wide-open veldt with the blue African sky high above my sun-bleached hair. Jungle gyms grew naturally from seed and were shared with the wildlife. I wore shoes under protest and then only to school or church. I needed a bath every single evening.

I served as an operational medic for two years in the late eighties and treated all kinds of trauma from arrow strikes to gunshot wounds. I've swum in the crocodile-infested Okavango and seen entire villages succumb to malaria. I have hunted poachers and listened from my sleeping bag to lions prowling and roaring beyond the firelight.

Life is a little tamer now. I live with my wife in the English countryside travelling the canals and rivers of England in a Seamaster named Wyebourne. Who knows, you might, if you take a walk along a towpath, see me on deck tapping away at my keyboard as I write about the very ancient past and the heroes of those times.

As always, happy reading!

Printed in Great Britain
by Amazon

84434309R00103